Tu hi Durga, tu hi Aminah aur tu hi hai Mariyam,
Tu hi mamta, aur shakti ki pehchaan ho tum,
Sukh -shanti aur aman ki pribhasha ho humdam,
Desh ki pragati, unnati aur abhimaan ho tum!!

Na tu jhukhna, na tu rukha, Aakhon ko na karna namm,
Dharti ho ya, ho aasmaan, Sashakht tu chalna hardam,
Maati ki khushboo, har ghar ka swabhiman ho tum,
Tuhi Durga, tuhi Aminah aur tuhi hai Mariyam!!

"An incredible story of women empowerment."

- Himanshu Rai, bestselling author of My Mute Girlfriend & I am always here with you.

"A beautiful book which tells a meaningful story about characters who are strong and lovable. A book which would push you to become a more socially responsible person.Go for the book, you would love it."

- Charu Vashishtha GulatiAuthor of Amazon Bestseller "The Lady in the Mirror"

Shield Maidens is a delightful concoction of adventure and intrigue that keeps you hooked till the end. Brilliant first attempt.

- Tarun Gautam, Author of popular novel, Rewind and Play.

Shield Maidens is a powerful work of art. It's contemporary and I was totally intrigued by the writing. Loved it to the core.

- Tanmay Dubey, Best Selling Author of Just Six Evenings, The Amigos, The RED LINE and DNA of a Champion Sales Person

"Jhimli's book is full of romance, comedy, drama and a strong feminist stand presented through modern Indian women. The book will definitely keep you hooked till the very end."

Kavya Sharma Author, To Naddiyaa

the shield MAIDENS

(Trio Cover Page Warriors)

JHIMLI PARUI

INVINCIBLE PUBLISHERS

First Printing: 2020

ISBN: 978-93-89600-34-6

Invincible Publishers

Registered Address: 201A, SAS Tower, Sector 38, Gurgaon - 122003

Edited by Chandni Mathur

Acknowledgement

First and foremost, praises and thanks to God, the Almighty for His shower of blessings throughout my work to complete this book successfully.

To my son (Aadhrit)

I just want to let him know that everything I do, I do it for you. Thank you for being a part of mine and making me understand motherhood.

To my better half (Prasoon)

Just a thank you would not be enough to regard you. I am grateful to God to bring you in my life and making me understand love and care. I just wish for you to be there beside me till the end of my life.

To mom and dad (Rama and Debu)

Without you, I would have been nothing. You have been the courageous parents who brought up a girl child and filled her with all the courage and boldness to fight the world.

To my sis (Shiuli)

Love you darling for being there for me always. And not to forget Pradeep, who has always been a friend before being my brother-in-law.

To my in-laws (Ranno and Ashok)

I am grateful to God to have another mom and dad in the form of my mother-in-law and father-in-law. Thank you for being there for me always. Thanks too to Smriti and Pramesh for their love and care.

To my family

I have been lucky to get a family who has been always there in my ups and downs. Thank you chachajis–chachijis, brothers–sisters, sisters-in-law, brothers-in-law, mamas–mamis, masis–mausas, buas–fufas and everyone in the family.

To my friends

Friends are the ones who are there with you by choice. I have been fortunate to have a lot of friends who have been there with me, unconditionally. The "bachpan ke dost", my college trio, the Jyotians, college groups and the office groups. I want to thank you all for always being there for me.

To my teachers and mentors

I am thankful to all my teachers and mentors who have guided me to excel in my work and life.

I wish to extend my special thanks to those people who have been there with me during my journey of this book. To start with, Harendra who gave me a push to write. Mayank has been my biggest critic, grooming each chapter. Prasoon, my husband, whose ideas gave me directions. Himanshu, Tanmay and Charu my friendly inspirations. Kavya, my first editor.

A heartfelt thanks to the Invincible Team, who could make this happen–Chandni, Satya, Khushboo, Ruhani, Guru and Ajay.

Finally, my thanks go to all the people who have supported me to complete this book directly or indirectly

Jhimli Parui

Love to the next generation of the family:

Avya, Anika, Reyaansh, Aarish and Kiaan.

Prologue

She was running endlessly amidst the dense wood. Two men were chasing her. She was gasping. She wanted to scream aloud for help. But no one could hear her. Everywhere around her she could only see tall trees and rocky land. She was just rushing between the trees, hiding herself from the sight of the men. Dusk was enveloping the surroundings. The chirping of birds was getting louder. She was praying for her life.

The two men had weapons in their hand and they were following her. They were sure to get her and their furious facial expression showed, they were going to cut her down with their swords.

She was wearing a salwar-suit and her cotton duppatta was dragging down behind her and finally got stuck in bushes. She turned around to give it a pull but it had got anchored badly in the thorny bushes. She could see the men rushing towards her. She had to get rid of her duppatta over there and leap forward to save herself from them.

Tears were rolling down from her eyes. She wiped them with her palm and paced herself. She was getting tired but didn't want to give up. But her left shoe got torn which made her trip. She was unable to balance herself and fell down. She held her shoe in her hand but it was more tired than her. She threw it away. She took off the other one and aimed it on the men who were still following her. Now, she was running barefoot. Her will power was not allowing her to pause; she still wanted to move on. She staggered through the rocky land, holding her ground to prevent herself from tumbling down. After a few steps, she started getting blisters and cracks in her feet, which were making her loose hope.

The two men jumped up towards her and pushed her from behind. She fell face first, rolled and collapsed. She kept sliding down but they caught up with her. She joined her hands and cried pleading for rescue.

One of the men swayed his sword and aimed towards her. She could not think of anything and she closed her eyes tightly to prepare herself for the oncoming swipe.

"Stop!!" There was a loud voice and she heard somebody giving a series of punches.

She tried to peep through the narrow slits of her open eyes but she couldn't see anything clearly. It was almost dark now. She could see one of the men lying a little away and another one beside her. She woke up with a scream.

'What happened, Gayatri? The same bad dream?' An irritated Richa turned on the bed towards her friend and roommate.

'This is the fourth night continuously since you have been having this same dream.' Richa showed her concern.

'There were two girls who saved me, but I could not see them clearly. I have to meet them for something good.' Gayatri replied to Richa.

CHAPTER 1

LAVANYA

A Sheaffer golden black pen smoothly flowing over the paper, held between long beautifully manicured fingers suddenly halted. The index finger with the pink base nail art slid over the text on the paper. It read:

**Name of Father/Guardian:*

**Name of Mother/Guardian:*

The index figure left the paper and went straight to a tricky itch on the forehead. It seemed like she was unable to understand something or was just a bit confused–her forehead wrinkled as an expression of the same.

The sharp eyes with defined kajal, thick eyeliner and smoky blue eye shadow blinked. She certainly had the kind of features that could easily melt anybody's heart. Straightened black hair caressed her fuller white cheeks. An attractive diamond nose pin shined on her straight nose. With matt mauve coloured lipstick creating an electrifying effect she was a perfect personality as a whole.

'*Excuse me, Sir*'

There was no response from the other side. It was a small room with limited furniture. An old table chair made of teak wood, a brown leather sofa adjusted with the back wall and two cupboards which contained piles of papers. A bespectacled middle-aged man sitting on the other side of the table was engrossed in some writing work. He seemed to be least bothered by who was standing opposite to him.

'*Excuse me, Sir.*' Her voice was a little louder this time.

'*Is this mandatory to be filled?*' She brought the form closer to the old man and showed the blank space.

The man pushed his spectacles towards his eyes and looked up, '*Hmmm...*'

'*But I am a single mother and she is my adopted daughter.*' The words shot like arrows and pierced the man's ears. The spectacles were carefully put down on the table and eyes opened wider. '*Where is her father?*'

'*I am NOT married.*' She mentioned with an obvious look since she already mentioned that she was a single mother with an adopted daughter.

There was pin drop silence for the next few seconds.

The two of them exchanged intense glares. The old man looked visibly unaccepting of this scenario.

'*Mumma,*' Pretty little Arshi said in her soft voice. '*Can I go outside to the play area?*'

The little girl's voice caused a sudden interruption to the locked eyes. The man was the first to blink before he uttered, '*You can go, my child! There is a governess madam over there who can assist you.*'

He abruptly called out for the governess who took Arshi to the playground. Arshi was happy running over the slides, swings and other activity created for kids in the play area.

The man then continued talking with the beautiful lady but he seemed to have lost his words. '*You look very young ma'am and not married... an adopted child... and...*'

'*Could you please tell me if I need to fill this in admission form?*' Her firm voice interrupted.

'*Just a minute, ma'am. Let me check with the Principal. May*

I know your name please?' The man asked.

'***Lavanya Sethi***', her voice echoed with bright confidence and dignity.

'*Hello Ms. Lavanya, please come*' said Mrs. Ragini Manchanda, the principal of Garden Blossom High School, one of the most prestigious schools in the city. Lavanya had come to the school for Arshi's admission.

The two ladies shared greetings and Mrs. Manchanda offered her to sit.

Mrs. Manchanda was dressed in a white and grey well-draped cotton printed saree which was matching her solemn and dignified personality. Her grey hair was neatly tied in a low bun. She was in her late fifties and looked exactly like a principal should of any well-recognized school.

'*You could have directly come to me. The office staff might not know you.*' Mrs. Manchanda addressed Lavanya. '*I certainly appreciate your courage to adopt a little girl in such an early age of twenties. I was following your court proceedings which were going around last year. I do admire the way you have taken it up against this social orthodoxy.*' Mrs. Manchanda knew Lavanya very well.

Lavanya smiled, '*It's your generosity ma'am. Kindly let me know how I can fill the admission form over here. Arshi is now three and half years old and I really wish she could get admitted to a good school like yours; it would be a deep obligation from your side if you could take her in your school.*'

'*You have set a new example for the society. These admission forms do not justify your case. I will get new forms printed. Thank you for associating with us.*' Mrs. Manchanda said with gratitude. '*Spare us a week. I will get the new forms printed and sent to your address. You can fill them and submit by next month.*'

'*Thank you, ma'am. Thank you very much.*' Lavanya greeted her and took permission to leave.

The gracious Lavanya in black trousers, satin blue top and blue Aldo stilettos walked satisfied down the principal's office. She went to the playground and called upon Arshi who came running towards her. She held her little arm while the duo walked down the school premise towards the parking lot.

***

Lavanya was driving back in her red Audi sports series R8, a car that many could only dream of buying when she got lost in some unconscious glimpses...

'*Ma'am, you are just 25 years old. Why would you want to adopt a one-year old girl? The honourable judge would like to know; are you going to take care of the child and of course what will happen if you get married?*'

'*My Lord!*' The advocate representing the Central Adoption and Resource Authority (CARA) screamed, '*Could you please ask the Petitioner to let everyone know, how she is going to meet the mandatory legal requirement for adoption which lays down that the age difference of adoptive parent and the child to be adopted should be minimum 25 years. She can adopt any other child who meets the criteria laid down under the law.*'

The courtroom had buzzed with murmurs. People discussed all kinds of things. Some of the leading newspapers and news channel correspondents were present in almost all the hearings conveniently portraying various views- best suited for their interests and channel TRPs. They knew that while some people secretly admired Lavanya's courage, some shunned her away openly.

'*Ms. Lavanya, if you can please answer,*' a firm but soft voice with immense positive volume emerged from the old man in his mid-fifties sitting on the judgment chair. He gave a firm and affirmative look to Lavanya.

'*My Lord! I humbly pray before this Hon'ble Court to*

allow me to adopt the child. I do assure you that I will give her all the motherly love and care. It would be my whole and sole responsibility to take care of the little one with honesty, reverence, love and finance. I am doing well and can commit to provide her with the required financial leverage. The little one will never miss the love and care of a biological mother. Her every need will be fulfilled. I can promise you she will be a part of my family and will be considered my inheritor. She will be given the best education and everything that is required for her upbringing will be taken up with full responsibility.' Lavanya joined her hands and actioned in a pleading voice, '*Please allow me to have my child with me. Please My Lord!*'

'*What about the law and rules?*' The opponent advocate screamed off again.

Since Lavanya was fighting her case herself, she pleaded, '*My Lord, I know there is a law to have the difference of minimum 25 years, but Sir, I beg of you and everyone in the society to please consider my case. I am now just missing out by 15 days. Kindly overlook that for the sake of the little one. Please...I request.*'

It was the final day of the hearing which had been running for the past 6 months now; the court had to come to some conclusion today. The news correspondents too were eagerly waiting for the verdict to come to some final decision.

Any general audience with Doon channels could find the news on-air echo newsreaders animatedly saying–*Lavanya, a well to do, young, smart and the most eligible girl, is going to adopt a girl child. What could be the reason behind this—A heartbreak or can she not have a child of her own? What would the judgment be since she did not meet the criteria of adoption and Juvenile Justice?*

The words like 'sterile', 'lesbo', 'cohabitation', 'privileged' were being gossiped upon. Sometimes this Target Rating Points and Gross Rating Points could get you out and make anyone narky. It's really scary for any normal woman to digest such filthy rumors being publicizedand left to a wide range of audience's interpretation.

But Lavanya was strong, bold and firm enough to break through the glass ceiling and stand up for what she firmly believed in—Herself. It's not like she was trying to set an example, but this had now automatically become a battle she had to win to prove something to people.

Lavanya had been pleading before the judge to allow her the privilege to become a proud mother. Many to and fro talks and arguments were filling up the courtroom.

'*Order! Order!*' Judge Ramanath addressed.

'*I have heard a lot and I would like to speak now. Considering the conviction and firmness with which Ms. Lavanya has put forth her arguments and keeping in view the welfare and best interest of the child, which is paramount as per the Juvenile Justice Act, this Court hereby allows Ms. Lavanya to adopt the child. This Court is satisfied that Ms. Lavanya is financially, physically and mentally capable of taking care of the child and providing for her in all aspects. However, to safeguard the interest of the child, this Court directs CARA to make bi-annual visits to Ms. Lavanya's house for the next 2 years and ensure that the child's interests are properly looked after by her.*'

'*Mom... mom...Ice cream.*' Arshi's voice brought her back from those background glimpses.

'*You want an ice cream?*' A smile followed on Lavanya's face after listening to her cute, little, innocent demand.

Arshi nodded.

They stopped by at the nearby ice cream parlour to enjoy their bites of ice cream; the mother-daughter bonding knew no bounds. The cold caress could be felt deep in anyone's heart and their sweet smiles sought by all. Deep inside, Lavanya was satisfied to know that she had not just won a court battle but a beautiful daughter in Arshi. Her world felt complete.

CHAPTER 2

GAYATRI

Richa opened the door with the keys given by her uncle.

'*Finally...*' Gayatri sighed. '*Hope everything goes fine now. What a long day it was!*'

It was around 5.00 P.M. Richa and Gayatri managed to enter the long-locked flat in the congested locality of Begumpet in Hyderabad. They had had a long and exhaustive day today. The girls had the takeaway chowmein and a breezer spritzer of pina-colada and cranberry each.

Gayatri dropped her luggage and laid down on the bed in one of the rooms of the reasonably sized two-bedroom flat.

'*The bed looks to be quite clean and nice, doesn't appear to have been closed for the past 2 years.*' A thought rolled down her mind. Richa checked her bag for a while, looking for a few papers, receipts and bills which kept her busy for the next half an hour.

Suddenly, Richa felt a pin drop silence in the room and her heart bolted as she sensed a presence around her who had come and sat beside her. It is a weird creepy feeling when you can hear each and every sound around you.

'*What Richa? Nothing's there...*' She murmured to herself.

She stood up and went to the other room and laid on her stomach and stretched her body. Her elbows cracked from being stiff way too long. She stretched her arms to relax and suddenly felt a head between them. She screamed and bolted out of her bed to take shelter in the corner of the room.

Gayatri, in the other room, heard the scream and sat upright in a jiffy. Concerned, she called, '*Richa*!!'

Immediately rushing to the other room she was surprised to see Richa shivering with fear. She found her couched up at the wall, her legs folded into her stomach and her hands covering her face. Richa was visibly sweaty. Gayatri at once embosomed her and wrapped her arms around her. '*What happened? Calm down. Shh... Calm down, dear. I am here.*' Gayatri tried to console her.

Richa could hardly speak anything. Suddenly Gayatri felt short breaths at the nape of her neck. Her eyes popped out as her tongue forgot to support her. She looked questioningly at Richa. Sensing the fear in Gayatri's eyes, all Richa could do was to nod to confirm her fear. They both were able to feel somebody walking in the room but could not see anybody. Both of them held each other tightly, their eyes wide open, and voices choking. They tried to close their eyes shut, probably thinking whatever it was, was nothing and they would feel better soon, but the eerie presence made them so uncomfortable that they feared that if they won't open their eyes, it may harm them.

'*Don't Fear!*' An unknown unseen voice echoed.

Gayatri and Richa stayed frozen. Their voices choked and they were unable to breathe. They had almost cut each other's arms with their fingernails while holding onto each other.

'*Don't fear, please!*' Again an unknown voice.

They looked at each other and before Richa, Gayatri gathered herself to break the silence and asked, '*Who is there?*'

'*Please do not fear. Are you guys able to hear me?*' Again the same voice asked.

Both of them tried looking in all directions but could not see anyone. It was just the voice they could hear.

'*Yes.*' It was Gayatri again. '*We can hear you.*'

Spookiness filled the room. Anybody in the world could have lost their senses to the atmosphere. Both the two girls, new to the city, new to the flat, at around 11 P.M. were couched lonely in a room. They were able to hear the voice of a boy but could not see anybody. Sweat pearls were rolling from their foreheads down their cheeks as if they had splashed water on their faces.

Richa was into a black hole. Both the girls were scared but Gayatri was more in control of herself. They were not able to believe their eyes and senses. Were they hearing something or was it their delusion? They were unable to believe their ears. They were scared of what was going to happen next.

'*That's so nice! It's been more than 2 years we have had somebody who can hear us. Are you able to see me also?*' Spoke the unseen, unknown voice and but now, a faded image was appearing. A young boy, around 7 or 8 years of age was visible as a faded projection standing beside their bed, smiling.

'*Oh My God! Help! Help*!' Richa started screaming and chanting mantras at the top of her voice.

Om Bhuur-Bhuvah Svaha Tat-Savitur-Varennyam |

Bhargo Devasya Dhiimahi Dhiyo Yo Nah Prachodayaat ||

'*Calm down sister. Please calm down.*' The boy started consoling them.

Gayatri asked surprised, '*Who are you? How are you here? Why were you invisible? And...*'

The boy ran away from the room, '*Mom, sisters can see me! They can see me!*' It was a happy voice.

Richa fainted looking at Gayatri speaking with someone whom she couldn't see.

Seeing her friend unconscious Gayatri's head spinned too and she also lost consciousness.

* * *

The Sun had risen and its dusty rays fell on Gayatri's eyes. The direct sunlight started disturbing Gayatri's sleep and brought her back into her senses.

Rubbing her eyes, she started shaking Richa, '*Richa... Richa... get up*'.

Richa woke up with a start.

'*Gayatri! Something happened last night or was it a nightmare?*' Richa murmured dazed. She still had goosebumps.

'*Don't know dear; let me check if I can get some tea or breakfast from the local market downstairs.*' Gayatri also was having mixed emotions, trying to re-collect yet be ignorant of it at the same time.

Richa said, '*Let me go and get it. You can take a shower so that we can leave for college early.*'

Richa and Gayatri were in Hyderabad, now Telengana, to join one of the prestigious business schools on Shankarapalli road. They were new to the city and Richa's uncle had helped them rent this house. They had decided to be in the flat till they got their hostel accommodation.

Gayatri could not forget what had happened yesterday. It was running over and over in her mind. Richa left for the market and Gayatri started her search in the house. She was curious to figure out why she could see that boy. She knew from the sound of the boy that it was a distressed soul. She possessed a special sense–'A third Eye', which allowed her to sense and identify any paranormal activity around her and now she could feel that she was here for some special cause. There was a heavy presence in the air, it felt laden and she could sense the pressing reality of a spirit around her.

There were some old newspapers in the house placed at the top shelf of one of the wooden almirahs. She pulled them all out to check and read. They were around 2 years old. One of the newspapers had an article with a circled headline that read as 'Double suicide in a house in Begumpet'. The article had some information that widened Gayatri's eyes. It read that House No D3–1304 in Begumpet encountered the suicide of a woman and her 7 year old child. Police could not find any other clue but a note which said the the lady had a fight with her husband and under that distress she had killed her son and slit her own wrist.

Gayatri stood up and spoke aloud, '*Hello ...Hello...Please let me know if I can help you.*'

She started roaming in the living room area, then the bedroom and then the balcony. She also checked the kitchen and the two washrooms. While wandering she kept on speaking and mentioning that she was there to help. As she turned a corner, her eyes rolled up with the vision in front of her. What she saw was unbelievable. She could see a lady wearing a blue saree and a boy holding her hand; the same boy whom she had seen last night.

Gayatri froze at her spot and developed a sudden abnormal gait, lurching and waddling and finally a pull of gravity. It was as if her feet were stuck to the ground.

'*Why you are here? I read the article in newspaper. Is it related to you?*' Gathering her guts, Gayatri whimpered.

The shadow sat down on the floor and Gayatri heard her saying, '*Gayatri...*' She knew her name! '*This is not true, we were killed!!!*'

There was a knock on the door. Richa entered.

***

CHAPTER 3

ISHITA

Ishita, like the name suggested was a real beauty as if a heavenly nymph had travelled to earth to spread the celestial aroma of beauty. She was jovial, perky and had a witty sense of humor; her love for conversations could easily be noticed by anyone. Apart from this, she was a loving housewife. But the fact also remained that people somewhat regarded her as a bimbo, as someone who sometimes forgot to use her brains. Looking at her nobody could know if she did it intentionally or not.

She belonged to Bhopal, a town in the heart of India, and known as the better half of Mr. Singhania, a well known Textile Industrialist. They possessed a triple XL size bungalow in a posh locality of Arera Colony. The bungalow was a dictionary of Indian relationships, a typical joint family.

'*Ishita, please get me a cup of coffee, I need to leave for the factory.*' This was a call from Amit, Ishita's husband who was the youngest of the three brothers in the family.

'*Just 2 minutes, Amit.*' She travelled with the classy glass tray in her hand from the kitchen through the stairs to their room which was on the first floor of the bungalow.

'Can I have my *coffee, please?*' Amit was relaxed to see a nicely brewed coffee in front of him.

'*Choose one from here,*' Ishita winked pointing towards the tray with three coffee mugs covered with heart-shaped coasters.

'*Not again Ishita, please.*' Amit was in a hurry, traversing around the room to pick up his essentials to get ready for his work. He quickly adjusted his black leather belt in front of the huge mirror attached inside the room, hurriedly opened the drawer and took out his wallet thick of two thousand rupee notes. Opening his almirah he took out his handkerchief and then turned around as if trying to remember what else he needs.

'*Please... please...*' Ishita was now running after Amit.

'*Why do you behave like this Ishi? You know I am getting late, right?*' Ishita kept the tray down and blocked Amit's way. Surrounding her arms around his neck, she looked deeper into his eyes and said, '*I am not letting you leave unless you choose one*'. She started holding him tighter, and tighter and... '*Okay, okay... wait!*' Amit touched her lips with his two fingers and her bold red lipstick left its mark on the tip of them.

Amit then went to the table with the tray and chose the middle cup, and removed the coaster.

'*Oh! Noooo...*' He jumped back. A black tiny snake popped its head out at him. Once again Ishita had played a prank. At once the whole atmosphere filled with cachinnation.

'*Amit.*' There was a loud raucous voice from outside. It was Amit's father.

Soon the cachinnation converted into giggling sounds and she handed over the correct coffee mug with a kiss on his lip to Amit. He sipped it and hugged her with a naughty smile and immediately left from the room. She bolted the door after Amit left the room and puffed her hair curls from her face, '*Ishi babe, get ready for the kitchen show now.*' She murmured to herself.

She then took a bath and was standing in front of the mirror in her bathrobe.

'Mirror! Mirror! On the wall, who is the sexiest of them all?' She was posing and flaunting herself before the mirror with a round hair-brush in her hand. The hair-brush was posing as a mic for her. She pressed the red nose of her Pooh hanging along the edge of the mirror and the Pooh sang–*I love you, Ishita. I love you, Ishita.*

A broad and picture-perfect smile could be found on her face. Ishita was not sure how many women did this on a daily basis but she loved looking at herself in the mirror and admiring her personality. Saree was something she liked wearing and it was the day of wearing a yellow one. She took out her pale-yellow saree with shining mukaish work, and a plum maroon blouse. The blouse could cover only the front, the back had only one strong string tied upon which effectively showed her well-shaped back. The full cleavage of a 22-year-old was prominent from the chiffon blend saree. The diamond danglers were well noted and an expensive bracelet that Amit had gifted her loosely hung on her left wrist. This was Mrs. Ishita Singhania ready to move down to the kitchen, after a few pout selfies.

'Lakhan Kaka, what's for breakfast? My stomach is growling—I am really hungry.' She impatiently picked up the covers from the dishes and peeped inside and in that dropped the last one with a clang.

'Hold on Toofan mail! I am bringing breakfast for you on the table. Please go and sit, malkin!' For once, she obeyed. Laughing Lakhan Kaka brought some crispy aloo parathas for Ishita. The Toofan mail that she was; she picked one of the parathas in her hand, spread some mango pickle in a straight line in the center, rolled it up and started walking off.

'Don't call me 'malkin', I have told you so a hundred times, kaka. I am your little daughter; just call me only Ishita.' Lakhan kaka smiled at her.

She smiled back and started walking out.

'Ok, beta, but at least sit and have your breakfast in peace.' Kaka showed his concern.

'No time Kaka, I have to get some dresses for Nikki, rush to the market, then come back before lunch, she needs them for the event by evening at her dance class... driver bhaiya rush to the market.' She spoke everything in one breath and boarded her car.

[Nikki was her 5-year-old niece]

***

CHAPTER 4

HYDERABAD DIARY 1

It was a chilly cold night. The clock on the car dashboard showed the time as 1 AM. The wild Napoli Black colour Scorpio SUV whooshed through the silent highway. A middle-aged man was on the driving seat. At the back seat, there was a middle-aged woman and a young child of around eight years of age. The child was fast asleep. The woman was also half-asleep.

'Ma'am, we are about to reach Hyderabad. Don't worry, we will be safely reaching the Begumpet house in the next one hour. You can take some rest until then.' Uttered the driver.

Mrs. Sharma and her kid were travelling to the Begumpet house. Mr. Sharma was a senior government officer and had got transferred to Hyderabad from Guntur (about 5-6 hours away from Hyderabad). Mr. Sharma was to reach the next day along with his movers and packers.

The Scorpio SUV reached the rented house–D 1304, which they had with them for a few days until they got the government accommodation. Mrs. Sharma reached her current house which was on the thirteenth floor of the building in the most crowded area of Begumpet. The building didn't really look old but had an old rustic look to it with the off white paint. Mrs Sharma tried to have an overall look but it was too late to access anything- plus she was way too exhausted of the travel and the necessary evils associated with it. It was quite late. The sky was already dark and the city seemed to be sleeping in peace. Hyderabad gets quite chilly during nights. Mrs Sharma vigorously rubbed both her palms together and spoke to the driver.

'*Where would you go now? It's late; you can sleep in the car and go early morning.*' She was a kind lady.

Mrs. Sharma had already seen that flat earlier and she brought the necessary items with her that she needed for immediate use. She made Samit, her son, sleep in the bedroom and asked Rakesh to prepare some tea. The apartment was a fully furnished one. The required furniture and kitchen items were already in place. Rakesh took the luggage in and took out the necessary ingredients for preparing tea. He got it ready and holding the tray reached outside Mrs. Sharma's room.

But right before knocking, he saw through the little door that was not completely shut. Mrs. Sharma was changing her clothes. She had just taken a shower and her semi-wet naked back was completely visible to him; he shivered thinking about her body. Mrs. Sharma was a voluptuous woman with an extremely sexy figure. There were goosebumps on his arms and something within him changed.

He finally knocked on the door, '*Ma'am, your tea.*'

She opened the door after dressing up, '*Keep the tea on the dining and you can leave.*'

'*Yes, ma'am*', but Rakesh was totally out of his senses, he just wanted to touch, feel and hold what he had just seen. Mrs. Sharma's naked back kept on flashing in front of his eyes and now he badly wanted to satisfy his instincts.

He had always been an admirer of her beauty. She wasn't aware but he had been peeping into her room at every opportunity to get a glimpse of her beauty but had he never got a chance to see her this close. He felt as if he had got a personal insight into her life. Mrs. Sharma came out to the living room to have some water. Rakesh could not control himself. His head was spinning with desire. He was thinking that he would never get such a chance and his brain supported his instinct. Rakesh has known Mrs. Sharma for almost 5 years now and had always had his eyes on her. Mrs. Sharma never realized this; she always treated Rakesh as a brother and had even helped him financially many times. Rakesh was getting fidgety, thinking of the wide range of possibilities in such a situation, this occasion wouldn't come again. He thought of all kinds of things except for the consequences- his mind had taken him too far away to think reasonably. All he knew was that he would probably never find her alone like this.

Having lost his ability to think sanely, Rakesh went behind Mrs. Sharma and enveloped her in his arms. He groped her from her serpentine waist.

Mrs. Sharma was shocked. She regained her senses and shouted at him, '*Leave me Rakeshhh! What are you doing?*'

'Ma'am I can't. You are so sexy and I have always imagined you in my arms. Oh! How long have I waited for this moment! You smell so magical, your touch is like a high voltage shock. I just want to have a happening moment with you.' Rakesh became crazier.

'*Have you gone crazy? Leave me right now!*' Mrs. Sharma screamed in anger.

She kept trying hard to release herself from his hold but Rakesh had gone monsterous. He tightened his grip around her waist and dug his nails in her flesh while all the time he kept rubbing his face on her back.

Mrs. Sharma screamed out of despice. '*What nonsense! Sharma ji will not leave you. How dare you!?*'

'*Sir will never get to know. We can keep it as our secret.*' A maniac obsession was taking over his sane mind.

'*LEAVE MEE!!!*' struggling Mrs. Sharma was trying to reach her room to pick up her phone which was put on charging.

She pushed and kicked Rakesh to release herself from his grip, but he was too strong for her. Rakesh was of a good built and Mrs. Sharma could not physically overpower him.

Hearing the commotion, Samit woke up and came to the room rubbing his eyes. He saw the horror happening in front of him with his mother and, gathering all his might tried to pull Rakesh off her. But Rakesh had gained a sudden insane power from somewhere. He stripped the boy off his arm and pushed him hard. Samit hit the corner of the living room wall and started bleeding from a cut above his forehead. He got unconscious and fell on the floor.

Mrs. Sharma screamed for help and gathered her strength to blow out a few slaps to Rakesh. She wanted to reach Samit. But Rakesh's mind was totally out of control, he took the knife lying on the dining table used to unpack the luggage and held it over her neck.

'*What are you doing Rakesh!?*' Mrs. Sharma got screamed in fright.

'*Stop hitting me, you bitch!*' Rakesh got really violent.

'*Samit is bleeding, please leave me. Let me go to him. Sharma ji would not leave you if he gets to know all this. You will rot behind bars, you bastard!*' Mrs. Sharma yelled with helplessness. She was unable to move as Rakesh got over her. With his right hand he held the knife across her neck and held both her hands behind her with his left one.

'*You bitch! That scoundrel can do nothing!!*' Rakesh was out of his mind. He gritted his teeth in anger. His face dripped sweat down his neck; he was breathing heavy and in a swift move taking the knife away from her throat he slit both of her wrists together with the knife.

At once, she was in a pool of blood. Rakesh got completely mad; he kept on slitting her wrist over and over and over. He was looking at the fountain of blood and kept murmuring, 'How could you slap me? How could you slap me, you filthy whore? I will not leave you.'

After some time, there was silence. Mrs. Sharma's eyes were wide open and stoned. She was not moving or speaking anymore.

Rakesh got back to his senses. He was sweating profusely. He started hitting his head on the wall with distress.

'*Oh God! What did I do, my darling is in a pool of blood. I just wanted to be with you and you hit me. Darling, I wanted to just love you and you hit me... See what that led to...*' His trembling voice was of a mentally insane person.

Now, he got worried to see her dead, '*Darling…ma'am, wake up, please wake up.*'

She was no longer alive to answer him or hit him. Rakesh kept sitting near her for some time, silent and still. Then suddenly, he got up with tears still rolling down his eyes.

'*What has this happened? What will I do now?*' He slapped himself a few times, '*What did I do? Oh God. I have to save myself now.*' That was all he could think of. He thought hard to come up with some plan. He became a suspicious detective and framed the scene of a suicide.

He made all the major arrangements. To start with he quickly wiped the traces of struggle; he tilted Mrs. Sharma's body and also cleaned the knife he had used to slit her wrists, putting it in her hands to put her finger prints and finally he killed the kid by suffocating him with a cushion. Since he was already unconscious it was easy to kill him. Within no time, the child stopped breathing. He then eloped through the balcony of the flat. The balcony was next to the stairs of the building. He just had to take the help of the window rods to get over there. He made the entire scenario to showcase that Mrs. Sharma had first killed her son by suffocating him and then committed suicide by slitting her wrists. He perfectly planned to put up a suicide note on the table, which said because of her yesterday's fight with Mr. Sharma, she had got upset and was ending her life. She did not want to leave her son alone; hence she was taking him along with her. Rakesh was aware of the argument that had happened between Mr. Sharma and Mrs. Sharma before leaving for Hyderabad and he used that as a tool to save himself.

It was an awful misfortune for Mrs. Sharma and little Samit. Both of them were lying in Mrs Sharma's blood. The mobile kept ringing; it was her husband, but she was no longer alive to attend the call. The walls of the house absorbed their screams forever. Little Samit had yet to see the world, but he had envisioned cruelty of the highest order. Apart from the two deadbodies, only flat no 1304, witnessed the horrible immoral misdeed.

The next day, neither the police nor Mr. Sharma could get any clue. The letter was discovered and Mr. Sharma had to admit that they had fought. Rakesh, the culprit was with Mr. Sharma all through the investigation and misguided everyone about the incident. He remarked that Mrs. Sharma was upset all the way and he had dropped them at the flat and left back for Guntur. He knew that if he ran away, he will be caught, so he preferred staying and playing his own game.

Rest was there in the newspaper which Gayatri had already read. Her mobile buzzed. Gayatri got out of her thoughts. She could not visualize if it was a real scene or she was daydreaming. But her brain was wide awake to make out that she was there to help Mrs. Sharma and little Samit. And she could sense that she had landed here for some noble cause. She woke up and tried to look around the house. It resembled the same as the one she had dreamt of. Now there was complete silence. The feeling of distress, concern and dismay was floating inside goodness gracious, Gayatri Deshmukh.

CHAPTER 5

HYDERABAD DIARY 2

Gayatri was in her college library. The things that happened a day before were disturbing her mind, body, and brains. Although she had had past paranormal experiences but she still tried to relate this incident to the real world. Richa kept a close assiduity over Gayatri but could not understand her confusion.

Richa was concerned about her friend. '*Gayatri, are you okay? You seem lost. I hope you are not still thinking of those as a supernatural dilemma. My solitaire, just fuck those thoughts off.*'

Gayatri didn't respond to that but asked instead, '*Richa, do you know the broker who rented us the flat?*'

'*Gayatri, please...no...we are not going to enquire.*'

Gayatri pulled Richa up and they took their friend's Scooty driving off to the broker's place who had got them the flat.

'*Uncle, could you tell me who used to live in the flat before us?*' Gayatri asked the broker directly. They were sitting at a small tea and bakery shop in the crowded Begumpet area. The broker was a local resident of Hyderabad. He sat across them in a white dhoti and shaded purple shirt.

'*Why Chelli*? What happened, any problem, sister?*' The broker Anna** got worried.

*Chelli means younger sister in Telugu language and **Anna is elder brother.

Richa promptly replied, '*No, no, nothing much Anna. We just found a letter in the flat and wanted to post that.*' She tried to handle the situation. On one hand, they wanted to know the fact and on the other, they did not want to lose the flat.

'*I will have to find it. The flat is very good; you should not have any issue.*' Anna tried to convince them and both of them had to return broken-hearted.

Broker Anna wiped the droplets of sweat from his forehead. Though Hyderabad is quite warm in afternoons, but this sweat wasn't because of the weather. Anna could understand that there was some issue. He ignored and did not come up with anything.

In his heart, he feared losing the commission which he had received after two years. That house had been such a headache- a waste of property for these 2 years. He was aware that no one can stay in that flat for more than a day or two. This was a pattern which had got repeated everytime.

Gayatri could understand that he was hiding something. She knew it would not be easy to get information out of him. But she chased him persistently almost every day. After around 5 days of multiple visits, one day, Anna himself called Gayatri. '*Gayatri sister, can you meet me today evening?*'

'*Of course, Anna, did you find anything?*' Gayatri was curious to know.

That evening, they both were at Anna's Begumpet office.

'*Actually sister, there has been some mishap in the house and after that no one took it, it's you who came in after 2 years. I hope you are fine in the house.*' Anna said worriedly.

'*We are fine but can you please give us the previous occupant's address or contact number?*'

Richa was curious. '*And why are you telling us all this now. Why did you not tell us earlier? Do you know what we were going through?*'

Gayatri knocked on her knee with hers to hush her. There was a lot more that they needed to know. Getting agitated was not going to help.

Anna said, '*Sister, I am sorry. I can refund you the brokerage charges but please do not inform the police.*'

Richa was not one to stay calm. She asked, '*Why not? What had happened there?*'

Anna was sounding scared when he said, '*Last night I dreamt that you were getting me arrested by the police. Please forgive me. I hid the facts from you just for the sake of renting that flat. I did not have any intention of troubling you, please forgive me.*'

Gayatri could at once sense that she was being guided. On the contrary, Richa was clueless.

Anna opened his creaking drawer. He pulled out some old registers and searched for the tenant details for that flat. After a few flips and turns, he said, '*Yes, here it is. He was Mr. Om Prakash Sharma, but I only have his mobile number. He was supposed to move to Hyderabad from Guntur but after the incident, he did not come over.*' Anna handed over the mobile number to the two young ladies.

***

That evening, both of them were sitting in their thirteenth-floor balcony. Rays of the fading sun were creating a mesmerizing effect. There were a few birds in the sky that was a mix of deep orange and dark blue. Nature's aura was glowing up the whole sky. Richa requested Gayatri for a walk on the Necklace Road, alongside the beautiful lake of Hyderabad. Their efforst were bringing in colours, as harmonious as those that lit the sky. They wanted to celebrate in peace.

Taking steps in unison *Richa asked, 'What are you planning to do with this number now?'*

They were brisk walking alongside the honorary green grassland at the bank of the most admired Hussain Sagar Lake munching on some delicious murukku.

Gayatri replied, '*I am not sure as of now. I need to convince him that I really got to know all this from his wife, and she wants it to be known to him.*'

Richa doubted it and asked, '*Will he believe you?*'

Gayatri was of the same opinion, '*I think we need to have real evidence for it.*'

Richa asked further, '*And how do we get that evidence, sweetheart?*'

Gayatri replied, '*Right now, I am really not sure. The only thing I know is Mr. Sharma should know what actually happened with his wife and son. He deserves to know the truth.*'

Richa suggested, '*Why don't you put it all on a paper and send it to him? Then it's up to him to believe it or not.*'

Gayatri reasoned, '*No, I can't do that, I have to make him understand each and everything that Mrs. Sharma wants me to convey.*'

Richa was concerned. She said, '*I really can't understand you. I will not stop you from anything Gayatri but just don't get too entangled in this story. Be safe.*'

The next day again Gayatri had a dream. This time she was to find the ring which Mrs. Sharma had indicated as evidence for her existence. Gayatri started searching for it in the walls of the living room, where it should be according to her dream. She ran her hand from the middle of the wall to the base of it to find anything unusual. Mrs. Sharma had showed her a crack in the wall in the dream, where her ring had got stuck that day. Nobody had recovered it till now.

She looked everywhere in the living room to find out the crack. When she was looking behind the wooden table, she found a patch that seemed to be recently plastered and painted. She looked around and found a pair of scissors lying on the side table. She picked it up and started poking the wall with it. The plaster started to come off. A hole was building in the wall. To her surprise she discovered a diamond-studded gold ring behind the soft plaster.

'Richa...Richa...I found the evidence!' Gayatri screamed with joy.

Gayatri gathered all her courage and dialed Mr. Sharma's mobile number.

'Hello! Sharma here.' A husky low male voice echoed.

'Hello Sir, good morning. This is Gayatri and I have something urgent to tell you. If you can spare some time and visit Hyderabad it would be really helpful. There is some important information to share with you regarding your wife and son, Samit.'

Gayatri's voice travelled through every nerve of Mr. Sharma and he could only say, 'Okay, tomorrow evening 5 P.M. near Salarjung Museum.'

Mr. Sharma was also getting some dreams about Mrs. Sharma and Samit. But he was clueless what they were indicating. He was ignoring them thinking that this might just be nostalgia hitting him hard. He could not even understand, why he said yes to meeting Gayatri. Well, he would always be affirmative for anyone who could tell him anything about his wife and son. And it had been long somebody had spoken about his wife and son. He was in tears after he dropped the call and could think only about them. During these years, there was not a single moment when he had not thought about his son. In his present condition Gayatri was like an angel for him who called upon his son's name after such a long gap and now all he wanted was to know what was it that she wanted to talk to him about.

Gayatri wrote everything in a letter and waited at the gate of the museum at the pre-decided time. She saw a white Innova coming towards her. The car was marked with a Government of India sticker. She was pretty sure it was Mr. Sharma. The car stopped in front of the gate and a man in his mid-forties stepped out of it and came to her, *'Hello! I am assuming you are Gayatri?'*

'Yes sir, I am Gayatri.'

'Hope you need not have to wait long.'

'*Not at all, Sir. I am glad you could make it.*' Saying so she handed over the letter to Mr. Sharma.

He took the letter, thanked her and turned to leave.

'*Excuse me, Sir. I have something else for you.*' Gayatri handed over the diamond-studded gold ring to Mr. Sharma, which she had found in the room. Mr. Sharma was taken aback, astonished to say the least. He was looking at this ring after 2 years.

'*I met her and she said she loves you. It was not because of you.*' Gayatri said softly to Mr. Sharma.

Mr. Sharma could not believe his ears. He had goosebumps through his body. All these years, he cursed himself to be the reason for his wife's eternal rest. A mixed feeling was running inside Mr. Sharma. His mind could not absorb this but his soul was eager to know. His heart was thudding in his throat.

'*You really met her!?*' There were tears in his eyes.

Gayatri held his hand in hers and tried to comfort him.

'*Please read it.*' She pointed to the letter which she had handed over to him.

Once glance at the piece of paper and an array of tears flowed down his eyes. His eyes got blurry before he could start reading. Mr. Sharma looked upon her with gratitude and admiration. He dug his face in the paper and sobbed his heart out. Having no idea what had happened, he had spent these 2 years in utter guilt. Many emotions at once engulfed him; he was relieved and angered.

He had too many questions in his mind. Suddenly that day flashed in front of him; his wife and son leaving together in the car. He thanked Gayatri numerous times for bringing out this truth. Somehow, just somehow, he completely believed Gayatri.

Gayatri looked at him and said, '*Uncle, she wants you to*

get the culprit punished. She wants to file a case against Rakesh, your driver.'

Mr. Sharma: '*What!! Rakesh!! My driver!! I have been so foolish; I should have questioned him more. How could I believe his words? That's why he left the job soon after. I am not going to spare him. I would get that bastard punished. He would definitely have to pay for it. I would not let him go like this. That bloody…!*'

Gayatri gave a consoling look, '*She still loves you and your son still misses you. Please do not take the guilt upon your shoulders but get that Rakesh punished.*'

Mr. Sharma broke down in tears, '*How could I let this happen? I should not have left them to travel alone that day. I should not have...*'

Gayatri solaced him with her words, although it was real misery and crippled affliction for him.

Mr. Sharma's eyes got red with anguish about Rakesh but on the other hand, he also felt fortunate to know the truth which would help him to lead the rest of his life with some contentment. It felt deeply obligated to Gayatri.

A sense of satisfaction and relief was on Gayatri's face. She was satisfactorily able to convince Mr. Sharma.

Gayatri realized that she had moisture in her eyes as she felt the presence of Mrs. Sharma and Samit standing next to her.

Samit's cute face wore a lovely smile and he was waving at her.

***

CHAPTER 6

MARRIAGE PROPOSAL

It was a sunny morning in Dehradun. When the gleam of the Himalayan mountain of Mussorie fell on the surface of Dehradun streets, they brought in the sparkling aura of diamonds and glitter. Golden streaks of rays enhance the glory of Dehradun. Such a mesmerizing allure can charm anyone. Lavanya loved to sit on her recliner placed in her green balcony and sip her black honey-lemon coffee daintily. She was someone who could admire the white snow peaked mountains of the Himalayas the entire day. Her glorious and strong glare towards the mountain ranges captured each and every glimpse of the natural beauty deep into her heart- she savored it all. All of this made her calm and brought her some level of peace. Lavanya enjoyed sitting alone in her balcony and relishing the beauty of nature. Her bungalow was in the least crowded colony of Rajpur road, and from her balcony, the fascinating view of Himalayan ranges could be viewed perfectly.

She was from a well to do Punjabi family who owned a chain of popular jewellery showrooms in Dehradun. She herself was a jewellery designer by profession and was well known in the city and even overseas. Apart from jewellery designing, she was a tech savvy woman. Software, coding, hacking and kernel programming was her hobby. She was the youngest of three children and had contributed to expanding their brand of '*Shubh-Labh Jewellers*' even abroad.

The whole city knew her by her name and also for her

generosity. She could boast about her courage to adopt a girl child, even though being an unmarried young woman in the Indian society and that too belonging to the small town of Dehradun. She was amongst those, who liked taking up such challenges which would make her stand out from the rest of the women in the country and her headstrong attitude favored her in this endeavor.

Her attitude was, '*Teri aisi ki taisi! (Do hell with you!)*' for whosoever came in her way of righteousness. She used it as chant. It gave her '*taaqat*'; strength. For her, *every moment is the right moment to do the right thing.*

Her father and brothers managed the three showrooms which they own in Dehradun. Her mother like any typical Indian mother would worry about her rebel of a daughter and say, '*Pata nahi is ladki ka kya hoga, kaun karega isse shaadi?*' [Don't know what will happen of this girl, who would marry her?]

'*Shaadi... Groom... other family...* ' These were the only meaningful elements present in her vocabulary according to her.

The only friend she had in her family was her elder sister-in-law (*bhabhi*). She was the one who always supported her for Arshi and of course her dad, Mr. Sethi, for whom his daughter was his heart and soul.

***

Lavanya had her routine fixed, it started off with yoga. Then a mug of black coffee with honey and lemon along with her friend, the Himalayan ranges. Like any other day, she was relaxing on her couch which was placed at the corner of her balcony providing a perfect view of the natural mountain ranges. The size of her balcony was almost the size of a room with a rare collection of plants and greenery. Such a view actually perked her up to start her day on a healthy and positive note. But that day, her morning had become special; her mom could finally initiate to welcome a boy and his family for lunch. She expected the boy to be her prospective groom. Her mother wanted Lavanya to be at home to acquaint with the boy.

A huge tornado of thoughts was surfing through her mind while she was trying to sip her coffee. The phone beeped. It was a Whatsapp message.

Then a to and fro conversation on the message started.

'*CCD @ 4 p.m. in the city?*'

'*Not sure*'

'*Why?*'

'*Guests are coming to meet me.*'

'*I am sorry sweetie.*'

'*Believe me so am I.*'

'*Ok, whatever you feel like. I will be waiting for you.*'

'*Hmm...*'

This word '*hmm*' in Whatsapp has enormous meaning. It is really difficult to judge what it may mean; it can be assertive, or just a surprised exclamation, or it can even mean a pause...so no more messages please or it can also say, '*Hold More Messages.*' It is sometimes so hard that you are confused if it is to say a '*bye*' or to take a pause and change the topic.

But Rachit replied, '*I still love you babe!*'

Rachit was Lavanya's boyfriend who lived nearby, he was like her soul mate. Although they lived nearby, they had got to know each other only recently. Being from different castes, he was less welcomed at Sethi's residence. Also, Lavanya had restrictions on her and was refrained from visiting Rachit's family.

So caste...let's recall something, if we look at its dictionary meaning, it says is, any of the social division in which Hindu society has been divided traditionally, each section having its own privileges and limitations, transferred by inheritance to the next generations is caste. But if we mean it actually or rather practically, it is a barrier which brings in emotional blackmails, social pressures and '*bhookh hartaal*' (relay of fasting on protest). Well, don't confuse it with religion. In religion love stories can bring in riots and wars.

'*Lovely... Lovely...*' Lavanya's mother called loudly.

'*Please come down, the Khannas are about to arrive.*'

'*Yeah mom, will be there in another 20 minutes.*' Lavanya was out of her 3D visual effect which bounced out glimpses while she put down her mobile and jumped up from her couch.

The Khanna family were in for lunch along with Bunty Khanna who ought to be the most eligible bridegroom for Lovely aka Lavanya. Bunty Khanna was a pure Punjabi guy from his looks and cooks. He was pretty tall and well-built, wearing only the most expensive of brands in whatever products he adorned, be it the watch or clothes. He was the owner of a chain of restaurants spread over some major locations of Delhi.

The Khanna family got settled well in the living room, the usual chit-chat started and Lavanya's mother kept ordering the home servant to bring the tea, then cookies, then some other snacks she had prepared for everyone and the bringing in of eatables and beverages never seemed to end. All this while Lavanya spoke only when spoken to; she didn't really speak much on her own. Everything was going fine and usual, until, Arshi entered into the room.

'*Mummaa...*'

Arshi rubbed her eyes with her left hand and was holding a soft toy doll in her right. She was looking as cute as a doll herself in her pink and white cotton frock. She walked down with her tender little feet devoid of any slippers and entered the living room where everyone was sitting and landed on Lavanya's lap.

'*Oh! My baby, you got up!*' Lavanya cuddled her.

Mrs Khanna spoke, *'Such a cute, innocent little girl, who is she?'*

'*She is my daughter-in-law's adopted baby. Lovely loves her so much that she is around her all the time calling her mumma.*' Lavanya's mother said before anyone could say anything.

The only person in the house, who would hold herself back in showering her love upon Arshi was Lavanya's mother. She wasn't very happy with her daughter's decision and could literally make hundreds of false statements to get her daughter married.

There was a pin-drop silence for a few seconds. The silence acted as a digestive pill to gallop the words and digest them without even a burp. But sometimes, the digestive drops eventually do not help to digest and you need to jab your finger in your throat and vomit it out.

Lavanya did the same.

'*Excuse me, she is Arshi, my adopted daughter and I will be right back after feeding her something. She is hungry.*'

Bunty Khanna was left gawking at Lavanya with surprise and fear. He experienced mixed emotions and watched Lavanya moving away with Arshi into the kitchen.

Everyone else in the room went silent; Mr. and Mrs. Khanna murmured something to each other, while Lavanya's mother looked down with embarrassment. Lavanya's father sat as it is, not giving any reaction- being his normal self.

Lavanya peeped out of the kitchen and said, '*And please have lunch. My mom prepares delicious rajma-chawal.*'

***

CHAPTER 7

CAFE COFFEE DAY

Café Coffee Day has been a well-known destination for hanging out for youngsters from the day it started long back, 22 years ago to be precise. I would say CCD would have witnessed so many love stories, love triangles, love breakups, business deals, start-up stories, celebrations, proposals, hobbies, adventures...oh! The list could go on and on.

That evening there was another story going on in this very coffee house. Rachit was waiting for Lavanya. The clock was ticking to show 4:30 in the evening. The CCD at Dehradun City Centre was quite crowded- a lot of college going students got free from their classes during this hour and this was like a hot location for them to catch up and chill. Rachit and Lavanya usually met here. Rachit was waiting for her, sitting on a sofa right at the end, close to a window. He was fidgeting on this phone, wondering where Lavanya was, but there was no sign of her.

'Two Classic Cappuccinos, please.'

'Sure, Sir.'

In a few minutes, the waiter got two cups of coffee with heart-shaped designs on the froth.

A soft tune of old Bollywood music was soothing Rachit's ears. His love filled eyes were trying to look for Lavanya in every passerby's face while seeing through the glass panes adjacent to him.

'Main saans leta hoon, teri khushboo aati hai, ek mehka-mehka sa, paigham laati hai, meri dil ki dhadkan bhi, tere geet gaati hai...pal-pal dil ke paas tum rehti ho...'

Rachit started humming too. He was totally lost in this song sung by the great legend Kishore Kumar.

Rachit kept sipping his coffee thinking about his love for this girl. He was so engrossed in his thoughts that it took him a while before he realized that he was sipping from an empty cup. Although it was quite late but he still wanted to wait for her, just a little more.

'*Excuse me...*' He called the attendant.

'*Two more classic cappuccinos please...*'

Attendant looks at the table and says, '*Sir, you already have one on your table which you did not have.*'

Rachit smiles and says, '*No worries, let it be. Please bring two more.*'

Attendant smiles back. '*Sure, Sir.*'

Rachit went back to humming the tune and browsed his mobile to check for any messages from Lavanya. He found a picture of him with Lavanya was pretending to slap him and he was saving himself from it. A mild smile decorated his face. The memories they've had together were special to him, he depended on them and Lavanya for his happiness.

***

Rachit was driving along with his driver over the long hilly roads of Uttarakhand. He was coming back from some automobile exhibition where he represented his stall to advertise his parental car showroom. A mechanical engineer from Carleton University, Canada, he was back after his studies, to join hands in his family business of car showrooms and services.

On the way, suddenly the car broke down.

'*What happened, bhaiya ji?*' Rachit enquired.

'Rachit baba, it seems like the car broke down. Let me check.' The driver went out to open the bonnet of his Land Cruiser.

'There seem to be some issue with the carburettor. Let me look for a mechanic nearby.'

Rachit too came out to look at the matter and said, '*It seems to be an issue of overheating of carburettor.*

'Let me see if I can find some conveyance. You can wait here and let the car cool down for 30 min. It should be fine then.'

He was a man of good looks. Anybody could interpret that he was a spoiled rich brat. His wore ripped denims and a white T-shirt with '*Sab Moh Maya Hai*' written on it. His grey coloured, gelled hair with messy spikes and colourful Nike Snickers were quite prominent.

Soon they saw a state bus coming along the same way.

'Bhaiya ji, I am boarding that bus. When the car starts, please catch up with me. Bye, take care!' And he waved to stop the bus.

The bus was filled with villagers, most of whom looked at him with intrigue. He managed to get a window seat crossing over an old villager sitting in the alley. The old man scanned him from top to bottom through his spectacles.

When he couldn't control his curiosity, he asked, '*Did you meet an accident? How did you get your pants torn?*'

Rachit smiled, surprised and said, 'Oh, *no, no, these are not pants… these are jeans and it is just style.* '

It was the old man's turn to get surprised, '*Tile...what tile...and Jeen... what is that?*'

Rachit laughed and said, '*Oh! Yeah dada, actually I was trying to climb up my car. I slipped and my jeans…I mean my pants got stuck in the car window and got torn.*'

Rachit could figure out that the old man could not hear properly and so he stayed a little loud while talking. He felt it was better to just agree rather than argue with him. But the old man was full of questions.

Old Man asked, '*Are you a monkey?*'

Rachit (winked) and replied, '*Monkey, no*!'

'*Why would you climb up the car then?*'

'*My bad! I felt like a monkey and I climbed up the car and fell down.*'

'*How could the bananas be there on your car roof?*'

'*Why bananas?*'

'*You said right now, you felt like a monkey and climbed up the car roof. Obviously you must have found some bananas on the car roof that would have made you climb the roof.*'

Rachit scratched his head and said, '*Again, my bad! Yes, they got missed on the roof of my car, and I felt like having them and climbed up the car roof but ultimately didn't get them because I fell down. Tore my jeans…no…no, pants. I hope I can explain to you now.*'

The giggles turned into laughs from behind.

He turned back to see who was laughing when he found a pretty girl sitting right behind him. Her broad laugh was exaggerating her beauty. Black messy curls were waving over her face to enhance her charm. She was wearing a blue cotton printed top with a cotton scarf wrapped around her neck. Her bob danglers were waving around her cheeks with the wind from the window. He couldn't move his eyes away from her face. He felt as if Bryan Adams' romantic song, *Everything I do, I do it for you...* was drumming inside his head and he could only see her mouthing words with no sound, her danglers dancing close to her cheeks and her hair making some lyrical moves.

'*Dada, I will get them stitched, don't worry*!' She commented to the old villager.

Dada got satisfied and stopped questioning after that.

'*Hi!!*' Rachit came out of his fantasies when she waved her hands in front of his face.

This was the first glimpse of Lavanya to Rachit. It was

love at first sight for him.

Rachit stammered a, '*Thank you, thank you very much*' to Lavanya.

She smiled and accepted it.

Rachit began small talk. '*How have you been on this bus? I mean where are you going?*'

Lavanya (laughed) and replied, '*I am going to stitch your pants, I mean jeans.*'

Rachit laughed too and said, '*Oh! Come on! Please tell me where are you going?*'

Lavanya looked up and dramatically said, '*Where the mind is without fear and the head is held high.*'

Rachit mocked her and added, '*And where knowledge is free. Answer me please, lady.*'

Lavanya laughed, '*Going with the wind and stacking up bananas.*'

Rachit rolled his eyes and turned back from her to sit straight. After a few minutes, he again turned back, '*You don't seem to be from the village. Are you going to Doon?*'

Lavanya was finding this ride funny. '*Okay, let me give you a clue.*'

Rachit became more curious and his attraction for her doubled.

Lavanya said, '*Towards Moon, to be replaced by D. I mean the beauty of a girl. I am love girl to be translated in Hindi with k silent*'

Rachit stood dumb and could just scratch his head. She laughed looking at his confusion. 10 minutes later, Rachit got up and went to the back seat to sit beside her. She smiled, '*So you got the answer.*'

Rachit replied, '*Not exactly, but I can understand you are going to Dehradun.*'

The bus stopped for a tea break.

'Do you want to taste some authentic farm-fresh tea?' Lavanya proposed.

'Anything for you. You saved me from dada.' Submissively Rachit confessed.

Lavanya said, *'Come on, master.'*

'Rachit, I am Rachit.'

'Okay, Rachit.'

They both went down for tea. On the hillside, there was a small tea stall with an old man standing behind the counter. They took two kulhars of cutting tea and walked towards the hill cut corner, alongside a deep valley view.

The beauty of Uttarakhand could be felt from everywhere. Her long, cotton, printed, flaired skirt was blowing along the wind.

Lavanya broke the silence, *'I love travelling and exploring.'*

Rachit said, *'I would love to travel if you could accompany me.'*

'Are you flirting?'

'You only told me you are going to get my jeans stitched.'

Lavanya laughed, 'O*kay, okay, you solved the riddle?'*

Rachit gave her his version, *'For me, you are a love-girl and I know you are going to Dehradun'*

She smiled. Her riddle was solved. The Love Kanya– with K silent, when read together becomes Lavanya.

They both were back into the bus now.

Rachit was extremely attracted to Lavanya, he slyly kept on noticing her talk while he looked at her awe struck.

Rachit was about to ask something but his phone rang. It was Bhaiya ji. His car was repaired and was waiting near his bus. Rachit got up from his seat, pulled his backpack, extended his palm towards Lavanya to request her hand.

'Okay dear love-girl, time to go. I am Rachit, a mechanical

engineer from Canada but a total Indian at heart. I am with my family business of car showrooms and services in Dehradun and I live on Rajpur Road, lane 5, house no 325. I do wear ripped jeans and I wish if you could get them stitched and also my vulnerable torn heart. Would you oblige to accompany me in my car till Dehradun?'

Lavanya blushed and smiled. She held his palm and said, '*Lavanya*'. Rachit felt glad and they both informed the the bus conductor that they won't be going in it any longer. The old man sitting beside gave a loud applause to them.

Lavanya said, '*Do you know I stay in lane 4, how is that I have never seen you?*'

Rachit replied, '*Really? I might be busy collecting bananas from cars.*' Their laughter echoed the hills.

Lavanya raised her hand to hit him out but Rachit ducked and saved himself.

***

Attendant asked, '*Sir...Sir Do you need more coffee? You have already had six, out of which three are still unused.*'

It was 30 minutes past 7.

He messaged Lavanya on watsapp.

'*My love-girl, 3 cups of Classic Cappuccino are waiting for you since 4.30.*'

After two min, there was a beep.

'*Drain them. See you tomorrow morning at 10 at Mussorie farmhouse.*'

CHAPTER 8

MUSSORIE TRIP

Mostly on weekends, Lavanya used to make a trip to her bungalow in Mussorie–this also added as a change to her everyday life. That day she asked Rachit also to visit the place. She took her backpack and packed another for Arshi. Hers had a picture from Frozen. They both left for Mussorie in her Audi.

'*Mumma, I forgot my doll. I wanted to take it.*' Arshi's cute voice emerged in the car.

'*Not a problem, sweetie, we can get a new one for you on the way.*' Lavanya promised.

The road towards Mussorie was a lovely hill drive. The beautiful weather outside added more power and energy to the drive. On one side was the hill and on the other a deep green mountain ditch. Lavanya played her favourite Ed Sheeran song on the way. Arshi kept looking outside the window, enjoying the ride with her mother.

'*Mumma, Maggi!*' Arshi screamed when she saw a Maggi outlet.

Lavanya smiled and stopped the car. It was a small plateau where there was a small shop which dealt with roadside snacks, tea, coffee and of course maggi. Having maggi at such a hilly outlet and admiring nature's beauty from such a height felt amazing.

'*Bhaiya, two maggis, one with chilies and other without.*

And one coffee please.' They both sat on the wooden chairs and table placed over there for the clients.

The atmosphere was filled with clean and fresh air. Lavanya closed her eyes and arched her neck to relax, the soft wind gently touching her face. She enjoyed this alone time with Arshi.

Lavanya walked towards the valley side of the plateau from where she could view the Dehradun city from in between the green trees and plants. She stretched her arms and pandered. She wanted to absorb the energy of the atmosphere into herself.

'Ma'am, your Maggi is ready.' The shop owner broke her reverie.

'Mumma, it's very hot. Please blow on it to cool it.'

'Wait Arshi, I will feed you.' She quickly got up and came to the other side of the table and helped Arshi eat her maggi. She carefully picked up the noodles with the fork and blew it cool, before feeding it to Arshi. They both were enjoying their hot maggi. They would roll the noodles on their forks and take the bite and suck the hanging ones with loud noises. Their laughter knew no end. Every time Lavanya was with Arshi, she became a little child herself.

Taking a turn from Mall Road into a side lane, Arshi and Lavanya reached their farmhouse. Rachit had already there.

'Rachit uncle!' Arshi ran to him. Rachit took her into his arms.

'My little sweetheart!' He picked her up.

'Here are your favourite chocolates.'

Arshi grabbed them with a huge smile and ran away to her playroom.

Rachit hugged Lavanya, *'How are you my love-girl?'*

Lavanya replied hugging him back, *'Good and you?'*

Rachit winked and said, *'Not good, without you.'*

Lavanya smiled, '*Oh, shut up, you liar.*'

He proclaimed, '*I swear*'

She laughed and said, '*I really wonder how you are still so flirtatious.*'

Rachit laughed aloud.

Lavanya was looking amazing in her casual capri and a short sleeveless top. Her recently waxed legs were glowing white. She wasn't wearing any makeup and had left her hair open. Rachit was also in his casuals with cargo shorts and a t-shirt.

'*Kaku, can we have some coffee please? We are going to sit in the garden.*'

'*Ji memsaab,*' a feminine voice came along.

Kaku was a middle-aged lady who took care of Lavanya's farmhouse. It was a three bedroom bungalow with two rooms on the first floor and one on the ground and a nice green garden with lots of plants. There were two chairs and a table outside on the lawn and they sat over there. The farmhouse had a beautiful green garden with lilies, red and pink roses, sunflower and aloe vera plants on one side and palm trees on the other. The backyard was a huge five acres of farmland. The house was painted in complete white and followed the principle of minimalism. Kaku kept the house really maintained and clean. She knew Lavanya visited it often.

'*Why do you seem so upset? What happened?*' Rachit started. He wanted to hold Lavanya's hand but she snatched it back and burst out loudly, '*What do they think of me? Why would I have to get rid of Arshi for my marriage?*'

Rachit sat back and stayed silent.

'*It is really weird to understand, why would a marr required at her cost? I did not bring her home just to get for such obnoxious reasons.*'

Rachit was still quietly listening.

'*Why would I worry of what the bloody M*

of me? Just fuck off; I am least interested in giving explanations of my relationship with Arshi. She is my daughter and she will always be. For fucking marriage's sake, I can't hand her over to Bhabhi. I just don't like my mom in such scenarios. She becomes very irresponsible and insensitive and forgets that Arhsi was my decision and is my responsibility.'

Lavanya was interrupted by Kaku who had brought coffee for them. Lavanya took a deep breath and got up from the chair walking barefoot in the grass. Rachit got up and held her from behind. He wrapped his arms around her waist and kissed her cheeks. But Lavanya was in a bad mood; she resisted and removed his arms from around her waist.

'*Rachit please, tell me how is this possible. I cannot leave her. I have fought with the judge and the lawyers to get her and now I can't leave her because of the fucking social institution.*' Lavanya was clearly frustrated.

'*Come, sit*', Rachit pulled her up and made her sit. He offered a glass of water to her, '*Drink your anger and now listen to me please. You need to get married some day or the other.*'

'*So..?*' Lavanya was aware that her parents do not like Rachit. They did not want Rachit to meet her. And the same was with Rachit's family. Rachit's family also did not want Lavanya as their daughter-in-law; somewhere even they were not accepting Lavanya with Arshi.

Rachit continued, '*You are living in a society. You have to think about it as well. You can't just keep fighting with everyone.*'

Lavanya kept looking at him.

Rachit said further, '*Everybody loves Arshi. She is a sweet little girl. Bhabhi also loves her.*'

Lavanya kept quiet as she was willing to know his views. She had never tried to know what Rachit felt of her life and her situation. Rachit held her hands and in a soft convincing tone said, '*Maybe you can get her to some nice boarding school and keep visiting her and fulfilling all the needs; better education nd a better life. This way you can look after her and get married as well.'*

Lavanya interrupted, '*Why boarding school? I have not brought her to isolate her in some boarding school and leave her alone over there. I have brought her to give her motherly love which she, unfortunately, got deprived of at such a tender age.*'

Rachit brought her hands to his mouth and kissed her knuckles, '*But think of when you would have your own children. Will you be able to give her the same share of love as you will to your biological children?*'

Lavanya was quite clear in her mind, '*Of course, yes. How could you say this? You know I am not that kind of a person. If you think like that then you also have the same feeling as others. And in that case, it would be better that you move on. I would not be able to adjust with you.*'

Lavanya drank the whole glass of water and kept the glass back with a thud on the table.

She handed over the coffee to Rachit. '*I don't know what is in your mind but to me love doesn't mean sleeping in bed with someone; it is far more than that. If you think I am just that then I am not your love-girl, Rachit.*'

Rachit kept quiet and sipped his coffee, '*I think you need some time with your daughter. I will leave now.*'

He got up, gave her his charming smile and left.

Lavanya did not stop him. She wanted to have some time to think about herself.

Love has a wide range of definitions. Love is something that comes as an internal feeling. For today's youth, this inner feeling is to explore each other. So when this love followed by attraction develops for someone, it is obvious that the drag becomes more magnetic towards the bed. The intensity drives the inner feeling to touch and explore. And when this touch and sense becomes a regular activity based on biological needs, this love converts into care. In such scenarios, love is actually unconditional and just devoted care for each other. Lavanya was more matured in her love.

She wanted a partner who could understand her and care for her. She really loved Rachit but her maturity wanted the same understanding from him.

***

CHAPTER 9

SRISAILAM TRIP

Gayatri shifted into the college hostel. She was still sharing the room with her friend Richa. Richa was now used to her instinct calls. She now knew something happens to Gayatri and she could sense many weird things, closer to paranormal. She called her 'CW', a Complete Womania.

Many men have been curious about how could a woman sense all their good and bad deeds. How a girl can sense the disloyalty of her boyfriend? How can a wife sense about the lies of her husband without any prior clue? How on the earth, a mother can sense the pain of her child even from seven seas away? This is a real mystery, even to women themselves. Some things have no answers really. Well, if we Google, we can find various articles that talk about the miraculous senses which are quite high in women. Some scientists even say that Women's sixth sense can be explained by two facets; one is that women tend to have better bilateral usage of their brains which means that they usually pay more attention to the right side of their brain which is said to be associated with more intuitive perception. Second is that women are brought up with more feelings. They are considered to be tender and grown up with more hearty feelings, hence it has been said that they use their heart and intuitive senses before their brains. They are inclined towards more intuitive feelings and observational skills.

Although Gayatri is a woman with a sixth sense more intense than any other common woman, she was also mature enough to understand the power it had. She dealt with it maturely, not misusing any aspect of her personality.

***

It was a pleasant Sunday morning. Richa and Gayatri were in their hostel canteen. *'Hey CW! What's the plan for today? Let's plan a trip to Srisailam? It's just 200 kms away and Gaurav is also going there.'* Richa winked her eyes with a naughty smile.

Gaurav was Gayatri's boyfriend. They all were in the same college and studying together.

'Hmm... he also asked me for the trip.' Gayatri mentioned totally engrossed in her book while having her breakfast.

'C'mon, then let's get ready.' Richa pulled her hand.

Gaurav and Abhay were waiting for them outside the girl's hostel gate. Richa and Gayatri came out to meet the boys. Gayatri dazzled in a beautiful blue, flared dress and bouncy hair. She was giggling over something with Richa, who was dressed in a white T-shirt and blue jeans.

'Hey, see your heartbeat is coming along.' Abhay tapped Gaurav. Gaurav kept smiling and was happy to greet her. They all adjusted inside the white Innova and left for the trip. Gayatri and Gaurav were sitting in the back seat while Abhay and Richa were seated in the middle. The seat next to the driver was empty. Music was playing over from the dashboard and the mild car fragrance lifted the mood of the trip. Chit-chats were on, some poking and some playful teases. Gaurav and Gayatri were holding each other's hand and were deeply sunk into each other's eyes. They were deeply and madly in love with each other while Richa and Abhay were the fun element of the trip. They came up with many Hindi movie love songs and teased the couple. They unpacked some snacks, chips, samosas and cold drinks. The snacks were rotating from hand to hand. Some were moving from one's hand to another's mouth and cold drink sips from one's lips to the others. The whole trip was real fun with love

blossoming between the couples. The outside weather was exaggerating the romance with its drizzling droplets.

Gaurav was saying, '*Do you know Srisailam is very significant to Hindu mythology? Mallikarjuna Jyotirlanga is one of the 12 Jyotirlingas of Lord Shiva.*'

Abhay added, '*And the hills, Srisailam Dam and the amazing view on the bank of the river will definitely take our breath away.*'

Gayatri piqued, '*I love any place with greenery and a natural view. It makes me so happy from within.*'

There group started talking about the place and its natural beauty.

They came to a crowded and narrow road. The vehicles were progressing slowly because of a concrete bridge ahead which was in a bad condition. It could withstand only one vehicle at a time and that snailed the traffic movement. A sudden scream from Gayatri got everyone to an alert.

'Hey! *What happened?*' All the friends roared in a single voice.

'*Please save the people! The bridge is going to fall in some time. We have to stop the people.*' She just blabbered hastily. Gayatri started pushing Richa to open the door of her side to let her get down.

'*What nonsense is this?*' Abhay reacted.

'*What are you saying sweetheart? Calm down; nothing like that is going to happen.*' Gaurav tried to console Gayatri.

'*No, I need to get down and reach the bridge.*' Gayatri pleaded. Gayatri could envision glimpses of kids who were delightfully screaming in a bus till it went down the bridge.

Gaurav was unable to understand Gayatri's exhortation. But Gayatri persistently followed her desire to get down and help. She could not sit quiet and just be an observer. Their car was around 100 meters away in the long trail of vehicles. None of them could digest what Gayatri was saying, '*Kids...*

a glimpse... help... wrecked bridge...' But Richa was acquainted with Gayatri and her sixth sense, she knew Gayatri will not stop and if she has seen it then there were chances of something really horrible happening.

Richa opened the door and let Gayatri get down. Gaurav followed. Gayatri started running towards the bridge. On the way, she kept instructing every vehicle passenger to not blow horn and not to rush. She ran faster ahead, followed by Richa, Gaurav, and Abhay. Soon she reached the start point of the bridge, and to her surprise, she could see that a school bus filled with kids was about to get on the bridge. She screamed, '*Stop the bus, just please stop.*'

She jumped into the bus and reached the driver seat.

'*Stop the bus and take it in reverse.*'

The bus driver was offended. '*Who are you and how could you get inside the school bus? Get down right now!*'

The bus conductor held her from her arms and pushed her towards the exit door. Gaurav jumped into the bus and held the conductor by his collar, '*How dare you touch and push a lady like this?*'

'*Gaurav, please ignore and stop the driver from getting on the bridge. Ask him to move back.*' She pointed towards the driver. Gaurav in no time followed her direction; he could not get what she was saying but decided to support his sweetheart. He held the driver's hands and leaned over him to pull the key out so that the bus could stop. The driver got upset and pushed him back. Gaurav punched him hard on his chest. The driver was taken back, but again he tried to take control of the bus.

Meanwhile, a truck overtook the bus and crossed it over the bridge which was meant for only one vehicle to go through it at a time. The truck was overloaded with some steel and the moment it was on the bridge a sudden crash happened. There was a loud sound. Its tyres got stuck into the cracks of the bridge road. The inertia made the bridge to shake for a bit and then fall down with a huge crashing sound.

A stampede ensued. The shake was like a small earthquake which made the school bus's front tires sink into the cracked concrete. The sinking caused the bus to lean forward a little towards the cracked pit.

The bus driver jumped out of the bus when he saw that things had worsened. He just opened the driver's door and leaped out. Gaurav at once took the seat to hold the steering to control the bus as much as he could. He screamed, '*Don't move and don't panic.*' to the kids behind who had now started crying out of fear. He turned back and saw them holding each other teary eyed. He could foresee, if he starts the bus, it might create a vibration, which could make the situation worse. Gayatri took out her phone and called the police. She also called up Richa to not panic and ask people to move back and get the road cleaned to pull the bus back. Gayatri then alarmed the emergency towing service and explained the situation. Her next step was to give some instructions to Richa and Abhay to follow. She took help of the conductor and they both moved the load to the back of the bus. The bus was in such a situation that even an inch of movement could make them all fall along with the bus into the pit. She consoled the kids that they would be safe and she would help them out.

By that time, the conductor was able to open the emergency window at the back. The conductor and Gayatri started supporting the kids to move out of the back window one by one and Richa, Abhay and others assisted them to move out of the bus and gathered the kids to a safe point. The process continued for the next few minutes. The police were there within 20 minutes and there were news reporters as well. The police took it over from Gaurav and thanked him for his bravery. Then Gayatri took the last kid out from the bus and jumped out from the emergency window. The air got filled with a loud applause. The crowd greeted them with praises and claps. Gaurav also felt proud of his sweetheart. One of the reporters ran to her and congratulated her.

'*People are saying, you screamed and stopped everyone saying the bridge is going to fall, how did you get to know that?'* Gayatri felt numb as her heart was beating loud and the shivering was raising goosebumps on her arms, '*I just felt it.*'

Many news reporters surrounded over to take pictures and cover the story of the accident scene. There were talks about the government's negligence and about the wrecked bridge and how the small kids got saved with the help of a brave warrior girl and a few of her brave friends.

***

CHAPTER 10

THE COVER PAGE

The morning dawned with the sensational melodrama in three different houses located in three different cities namely Dehradun, Bhopal and Hyderabad. One of the leading women magazines [*The Women of Today*] highlighted the headlines as '*Today's women in breaking the glass ceiling!*'

The cover page was decorated with three beautiful faces -

Lavanya Sethi

Gayatri Deshmukh

Ishita Singhania

Lavanya's story of being a single mother and her ups and downs were brought up. Gayatri was featured for her brave act while she saved the life of a bus full of kids with her inner power. The maximum melodrama happened at Ishita's home. The timid, pigeon-hearted had been praised for her teachings on martial arts to women for self-defense. She was identified as the 'Black sash' in Karate and Taekwondo. Her classes were doing wonders not only in Bhopal but were getting popular all over Madhya Pradesh and Chhattisgarh.

Rachit called up Lavanya to congratulate her.

'*Hi dear! You are looking awesome on the cover page of the magazine.*'

Lavanya smiled and said a '*Thank you!*'

Rachit asked, '*If you are okay can I have ask for the pleasure of having lunch with my cover girl who has been a social princess warrior?'*

Lavanya laughed and said, '*Sure Mr. Mechanic cum Monkey cum Rancho!! Ha! Ha! Ha!*'

There was ballyhoo in the hostel with roars of Gayatri being a celebrity. She got felicitations and quick praises from her college principal and teachers. Her friends were boasting to others about being friends with her.

There were calls from her friends and relatives. The only blessing she was missing was from her mom and dad.

She was sitting alone after all these events in her room with a picture of her mom and dad. It was a great misfortune for her when she had lost her parents in a car accident at the tender age of 12. Post this mishap, she started getting an enhanced sixth sense. She could clearly recall the first time when she saw her mom and dad in her room while she was studying and she chatted with them and soon after she had received the news of their accident.

She was being taken-care of by her maternal aunt in Pune all these years. Her *Masi* had been her whole and soul.

The Singhania family was shocked when they started getting calls of praises for Ishita. The whole bungalow of Arera Colony was stirred. Amit was in a real shock as it was hard for him to believe that she was his Ishita who had got praised as the power woman in the magazine. He could not gulp up the fact that his mischievous jovial Ishita was a real hidden warrior.

When he had heard it first, he couldn't believe it. A colleague at work had come to him with the magazine.

'Hello Amit ji, congratulations! Bhabhi ji is a real hero. You must be really proud of her.'

'You must have been mistaken. She is not my Ishita. She must be someone else.'

'No Amit ji, it is bhabhiji's photo on the magazine. Have you checked the magazine–The Women of Today?'

Amit left his work and was back home in no time. Ishita was in her light blue saree and was lying down on the bed. She was talking to someone, although Amit could not exactly confirm who that was as she had put on her earphones. She saw him and was pleasantly surprised.

'*Why are you home so early today? Are you okay?*'

Amit, who was a little annoyed said, '*Yes, I am fine. What about you? Can you please stop this latest prank of yours? I have gone insane attending to calls since morning. Everybody is like, Ishita bhabhi is this... Ishita bhabhi is that...*'

Amit tried to mock away his confusion in front of her by fading out his anger into a smile.

Ishita asked him seriously, '*So, what do you think. Is it right or wrong?*'

Amit wasn't sure of an answer but said, '*Oh Darling, there is nothing right or wrong in this. This is you, my Ishita and they were talking about somebody else who is some black belt in Karate or something.*'

Amit came closer to Ishita and held her arms. Ishita looked deep into his eyes and asked, '*If it was me, then is it right or wrong?*'

Amit got blown away. A wave of shock travelled through his body and his hands left her arms. An astonishing look engulfed his face.

Surprised he said, '*You never told me about this.*'

Ishita said, '*I tried many times but my parents and your parents wanted marriage.*'

Amit slumped on the chair nearby, '*You did not tell even me. At least you could have told me.*'

'*I swear, I wanted to tell you many times, but I felt, you may also not like it.*'

'*Ishita, how could you...?*' Amit was sad and got up to leave the room.

'*Amit, please don't go like this. I really wanted to tell you everything.'* Ishita tried to stop him.

He screamed, '*Oh Really! Else ma'am will use her skills to hit me. Okay, come on, hit me.*'

'*I don't want to hurt you Amit. I love you. I really love you and I don't want to lose you.*' Ishita was in tears.

Amit pretended not to hear her and left the room. Ishita burst into tears. She sat down on the floor and cried her heart out. She could remember those days; she had had a fight with her dad when he did not want her to come out with the truth about her talent in front of her in laws and Amit. She wanted to share this with Amit but Ishita's family was afraid that they would lose the marriage proposal of a bride with martial arts. A girl who does marshal art might not be considered as a good marriage material and would be considered as a reason of confrontations, clashes and combat. The prejudice is, a good fighter would always like to fight and win, and would not be submissive to her husband to make a happy home. A common myth followed during match making, a bride should be timid and tender and the bridegroom should be bold and empowering.

Tu hi Durga, tu hi Aminah aur tu hi hai Mariyam,

Tu hi mamta, aur shakti ki pehchaan ho tum,

Sukh -shanti aur aman ki pribhasha ho humdam,

Desh ki pragati, unnati aur abhimaan ho tum!!

Na tu jhukhna, na tu rukha, aakhon ko na karna namm,

Dharti ho ya, ho aasmaan, Sashakht tu chalna hardam,

Maati ki khushboo, har ghar ka swabhiman ho tum,

Tuhi Durga, tuhi Aminah aur tuhi hai Mariyam!!

Ishita wiped her tears, got up and decided to tell the complete truth to Amit and his family. This was the time. She could not fake it anymore- she could not lie because this was something she had mastered over the years and she knew she was good at it. She was proud of herself and she wanted her husband and in-laws to be proud of her too. And what good would it bring to hide something from people you love? Fuck society and its expectations!

All this while she remembered the times she went to practice and teach the kids in hiding. This was her passion She really did want to make a difference.

***

CHAPTER 11

FEEDBACKS

Lavanya, Rachit and Arshi were sitting around a round table. They came down to celebrate Lavanya's achievements. Rachit ordered some starters; french fries in particular that were Arshi's favorite. It was Saturday afternoon. Being the weekend the restaurant was quite crowded- all the tables were occupied and there were people waiting outside for their turn. There were all kinds of people; families, young boys and girls and couples- everyone busy chattering their time away.

The café was on Rajpur road and was new. Lavanya and Arshi really liked the décor- there was a flower decorated cycle right outside the entrance- it was a small cozy café known for its Italian and Mexican cuisines. Beautiful handmade lamps hung from the ceiling, which gave a very warm and comfortable vibe and the round, wooden tables had comfortable chairs around.

Rachit looked lovingly at the little girl and asked, 'Arshi, do you like this place?'

A beaming Arshi replied, '*Yes, uncle, I love this place. But I can see swings on that side. Shall I go over there to play?*'

Lavanya stepped in, '*No Arshi, just stay here. Your favourite pasta would soon arrive.*'

Rachit sided with Arshi and said, '*Let her go. The food might get delayed. I would keep an eye on her.*'

Lavanya smiled at getting cornered. Arshi ran away happily to the play area which was just a few steps away.

Seeing Arshi away, Rachit took the opportunity to speak with Lavanya.

He said, '*Love-girl, I know you were angry with me from that day. I am sorry if I have hurt you by any chance. But I just want to say, you are my love-girl and you are the only one whom I Love.* '

Lavanya was quiet and listened to him without any reaction.

Rachit went on with his one-sided conversation. '*From the day, I saw you in that state bus, I have been in love with you. I cannot even think about anyone else except you. And today, I want to confess something.*'

His words alerted Lavanya. She looked up into his eyes. She was all attentive and suddenly eager to know what Rachit had to say.

Rachit put his hand over hers and looked straight into her eyes. '*I love you very much my love-girl. But I must say marriage is a little different. It needs a lot of commitment. It means responsibility, courage to take a stand and stay together to make things happen. It is just not about you and me. It is a connection between two families. We can't just think about one thing. We have to look around us and be responsible for all of our steps.*'

Lavanya got confused. She pulled her hand away from under his and crossed them over her chest. Straight faced she waited for what was coming.

Rachit kept looking at her till she lost her patience and curtly said, 'Come to the point, please.'

Rachit slumped back in his chair. He could not face Lavanya at this point. He just looked into oblivion and breathed to calm his nervous self. 'I am not ready right now to take any responsibility. I am unable to think about marriage at this time. I am really sorry.'

Lavanya questioned, 'Is this you speaking or your mom?'

Rachit got surprised at her question. But he answered, 'It's me.'

Lavanya asked the next question, 'Ok, so what do you want from me?'

By the time Rachit could answer, his eyes got glued to a group of ladies who had entered the restaurant. Amongst the group was his mother. It seemed they had come for their kitty party.

Lavanya could understand Rachit was getting awkward. He was trying to hide himself. She felt a surge of disappointed run through her heart. She tried to hold her tears and act bold.

She got up at once and walked down to call Arshi. She held her arm and pulled her to herself and came back to the table where Rachit was sitting.

She said, 'I need to go; the service seems quite bad and delayed here today. I think I should take leave. We can have lunch some other time.'

Arshi was insisting for her pasta, but Lavanya promised her an ice-cream to console her and walked out with her daughter.

Rachit was left feeling awkward. He was unable to respond or react.

While she walked out of the exit door, she crossed the table where his mother was sitting. She could clearly hear words like '*Lavanya…not the girl for my Rachit.*' She did not particularly feel bad about anything- she knew there were very few people in her life who actually understood her decisions. She was pretty sure the others were not in her favor but it had stopped bothering her now.

***

Amit was driving along with his mother in the busy streets of New Market. He was annoyed with Ishita that she had not trusted him. He was hurt. He had always believed that he was Ishita's best friend and she could talk about anything and everything to him. But he was proven wrong. Ishita had disappointed him by hiding from him an integral part of her life. He was lost in his thoughts when suddenly, he saw Ishita from his car window.

She was standing right across the road with a group of street children. When the traffic stopped, she moved the kids inside the gate of a tattered building. It had a dusty ground but it was big enough to house all the kids. Amit quickly parked his car outside the building and carefully walked to the gate. He could see his wife there with all those children. Several other boys and girls of average 12-16 years had joined the group. He hid himself but kept watching. Ishita was teaching martial arts for self-defense to around 50 children. Amit noticed how talented she was in what she was doing and how passionately she was teaching the kids. Although this time, she was not in her traditional saree but a black Nike tracksuit.

He slowly walked closer to the area where Ishita was teaching the children. There was a tea stall near the entrance. He hid behind the crowd near the stall that was gathered to view the training and ordered a tea. Ishita could not see him. She was occupied by all the moves that she wanted to teach the children.

Amit kept observing her. He was absorbing her each and every action deep inside of himself feeling proud of his young beautiful wife. He could see the adorable smile, the brightness of her eyes and the complicated moves she was carefully focusing upon.

Ishita was ignorant about Amit watching her. This was her usual routine. In the morning, after Amit left for work, she used to get ready, do her kitchen duties along with the help and leave home to take lecturers on self-motivation and guiding children about martial arts. She also taught them self-defense. It seemed that these children were from two schools for underprivileged children. There were kids in two different uniforms. Both the schools had given her an open area along with a few weight lifting equipments to work with, but she loved taking classes in the open ground.

She was trying her best to impart training to these teenage boys and girls. But this wasn't easy. Not many were interested in making their children learn self-defense, they hardly saw any point in it. Ishita had to convince them with love and logic. All this while, everybody at home thought that she was either going for her kitty parties or to her friend's place, so nobody suspected.

She was assisted by two other girls who were checking upon the children to see if they were doing it right. It was more than an hour now. Amit had gulped down 4 glasses of tea during this time. Ishita was almost done with her class. He heard her say the word 'ice cream' followed by a loud cheer form her students. She took all of them to the most famous Top n Town Ice cream parlour and bought them ice cream candies.

'Will you share the ice cream with me, ma'am?'

Ishita turned around to see for who was offering her ice cream. To her surprise, it was Amit standing in front of her with a chocobar in his hand, which was her favourite.

Her first expressions were frowned lines of her forehead. She was worried that Amit would get angry.

She stammered, 'I...I am…I was just passing by and offered the kids some ice cream… I am sorry.'

'Please don't be sorry, love.' He tried to calm her down and said, 'Do you know I have been watching you for the past one hour?'

Ishita sighed and took the ice cream from him to take a bite.

Just then Amit's phone rang. It was his mother calling. He picked up the phone and said, 'Maa, I am unable to come pick you up myself but I am sending the driver and the car to you.'

He looked at his wife's scared face and added, 'And Maa, I want to tell you something important. Ishita got featured in a very famous magazine. She was fabulous. When we come back, we will tell you the whole story and party at home. Also, I want to tell you that your daughter- in-law is a brave lady. She is a black belt in martial arts! I knew it since long but could not tell you. Today evening we will have a pizza party to celebrate her achievements.'

Ishita could not hear what her mother-in-law said but she saw Amit smile before he hung up.

Ishita's happiness knew no bounds. She dropped her ice cream and jumped to hug Amit. She did not even bother that it was a public place. When you are happy and your reason for happiness is in front of you, you do not bother about what people would think.

Ishita felt lucky to have a life partner like Amit.

Amit was far happier to have a sweet, jovial, bold woman as his life partner.

***

CHAPTER 12

HOTEL LALITA PALACE

'*Good morning, Sir. Welcome ma'am, to our hotel, Lalita Palace. How can I help you?*' Ishita and Amit were greeted by a beautiful lady, elegantly dressed up in a nicely draped silk saree at the reception.

'*We have a booking here for 5 days and 4 nights under the name Mr. and Mrs. Singhania.*'

'*Sure Sir. I will just check.*' She looked into the desktop that had been set up in the reception to update the mandatory details and then she handed over the lock card to one of the escort boys and said, '*Please escort Mrs. and Mr. Singhania to room no 607.*'

'*Sir and Ma'am, wish you a nice stay. We have our masked ballroom night at our banquet from 8:00 p.m. Please honor us with your visit.*' Ishita nodded her head and turned back to move on.

'*Excuse me ma'am...*' the receptionist called after her, '*Can I have a selfie with you?*'

'Umm... *Why?*' Ishita was surprised.

'*You are the same lady who got featured in the magazine last month, right?*' The receptionist confirmed which made Ishita come up with a broad smile. She then showed the magazine which was present on the table at the waiting lounge. Amit smiled and nodded and showed his consent to go ahead. The receptionist took the selfie and said, 'Actually I will try to take a selfie with all three of you. I am so inspired by all of you.'

'All three, how do you mean to do that?'

'*Ma'am, you would be surprised to know that Ms. Lavanya and Ms. Gayatri who shared the front page with you on the magazine are also there in our hotel right now. They checked in yesterday.*'

'*Amazing, I would also get to know them. Thanks for letting me know. And I think that's a brilliant idea. I would also get a chance to meet them.*' Ishita *was pleasantly surprised.*

Ishita and Amit were here to celebrate their 1st anniversary.

Gayatri had come with her friends for a college seminar.

Lavanya was here for a jewellery and fashion fest.

Coincidentally, they happened to get their bookings at the same time in the same hotel.

***

It was morning 10:00 a.m. and the sun was roaring bright in its full bloom and heat. Delhi was bright and hot. Gayatri got dressed in a formal light pink shirt with a pink printed scarf decently knotted around her neck and black striped trousers. She stood in front of the dressing area in her room and was engrossed in the mirror to apply black eyeliner. She closed one eye on which she was applying her eyeliner and kept her left eye open to check the correctness of the liner. All of a sudden she screamed, '*O! Maaa*!!!' and her liner got spread over her eye. Richa who was sitting on the bed and packing some papers in her handbag jumped up and all the papers scattered.

'*What happened to you, Gittu? Don't tell me you saw something again. I do not want any more mysteries here please.*'

Gayatri was in complete silence this time. She could not

believe her eyes. Richa came up to Gayatri, and held her shoulder, '*Are you fine?*'

She just nodded.

'*Let me know if you want to share.*' Richa took the cleanser from her kit and rubbed her eye to remove the smudged liner.

'*You can try now.*' But Gayatri ignored it and said, '*Let's go!*' And packed her cosmetics back into her kit box.

They both locked the room after them and left through the corridor towards the lift and then moved to the dining area for breakfast.

The dining area of the hotel was quite large and the sitting area was organized in the form of round tables with four orange colored sofa chairs to them. The breakfast had a buffet system with a variety of food items. Gayatri took her plate and reached to pick some vegetable mayonnaise sandwiches. There were also stuffed aloo and gobhi paranthas, sambhar, idli, vegetable poha, cereal, fresh juices, toast and a good number of fresh fruits. She extended her hands to get the tongs when suddenly someone else took hold of them. She pulled her hand back and turned her face to see who it was who had taken the tongs. She heard a polite sorry before she saw the face. Gayatri lifted her eyes, to find Lavanya standing beside her. She was a tall, fair and confident lady. She was well dressed in knee length pencil skirt and purple top and black ballerinas.

Gayatri could at once recognize her face; the same charm as was on the magazine's cover page. The same sharp features, with light pink lipstick and well-set semi curly, shoulder-length hair. '*Are you Lavanya, from the magazine's cover story of last month?*' She couldn't resist asking.

'*Yeah, and you must be Gayatri?*' Lavanya could also remember her innocent face with graceful beauty. At the back of her mind, Gayatri could relate what she saw some time back in her room while putting her liner.

'*It's so nice to meet you,*' Gayatri took the tongs, picked a sandwich and placed it in Lavanya's plate.

'*Same here. It's such a small world!*' Lavanya was happy.

Lavanya offered, '*Get your plate and we will share the table in that corner.*' She pointed to an empty corner table. Since they had been the popular magazine's cover page girls, some of the people were whispering looking at them. Gayatri and Richa took their food and walked down to share the table with Lavanya.

'*Where is your little one?*' Richa asked.

'*She is Richa, my best friend*', Gayatri introduced.

Lavanya was only aware that Gayatri had taken a brave step in saving the school kids during that incident of the bridge collapse. She had no idea about her overworking sixth sense. Actually, it was something that was hard to believe by anyone unless and until they experienced it on their own and same was the case with Lavanya. They had their breakfast together and had some swift chats and then they dispersed for their work with a promise to meet again in the evening. Lavanya booked a cab from the reception and waved a bye to leave for Pragati Maidan for the Jewellery fest. Gayatri turned around to find Gaurav waving at her and gesturing him to come over. He arranged for a van to reach the venue.

Gaurav was a handsome man with medium built and he was always well dressed. Today he was wearing light blue plain shirt and black trousers. A deep red and blue striped tie was hanging through his neck. He was looking very attractive; his face was cute and he had a boyish charm to him. Abhay was also equally handsome but Gaurav had an intellectual look. They both were waiting with opened slide doors of the van to comfortably get the girls into the van. Similarly, although Richa was prettier than Gayatri but Gayatri had simplicity in her looks and was more earnest and calmer than Richa which made her stand out in any crowd.

Gayatri got into the van and took the window from

where the other side of the road was visible. She saw two girls dressed in glittery, off-shoulder dresses with complete makeup and hairdo boarding a luxurious car. Though they were dressed like grown up women, they seemed to be young and tender in age. Her van moved but she tried to peep outside to watch the car and the girls till as far away as she could. Soon the car was out of her sight. But again, a visual glimpsed in front of her eyes and she shivered.

'*Gayatri, what happened?*' Richa held a shaking Gayatri from her shoulders.

Gayatri was zapped. She said, '*Richa, I don't know but I am feeling something. We are here again for some cause. But this time it seems to be far more dangerous than any other situation I have ever passed through.*'

Richa held her tighter and said, '*Calm down sweetheart, we will cross the bridge when we reach there. Right now just come out of it and enjoy.*' Gayatri controlled herself and smiled. Gaurav gestured Richa to swap seats and Richa happily obliged. Now Gaurav and Gayatri were on one seat and Abhay and Richa on the other. Gaurav took out Gayatri's favourite Cadbury's Five Star and offered her. '*This is for you, Gittu*', Gaurav smiled.'*My Five Star,*' Gayatri smiled and tried to grab it. But it was Gaurav; it was not that easy to get something from Gaurav. He raised it higher. Gayatri jumped, '*Hey, give me that.*'

'*Take it, it is for you only.*' Gaurav teased. Richa too was encouraging Gayatri, '*Grab it dear! Don't let him win.*'

Abhay was encouraging Gaurav, '*Don't let her win. You are my bro, you can't lose!*'

Finally, Gayatri got upset and said, '*I don't want it. Give it to that aunty.*' She pointed to a lady standing on the roadside whom she could see from the window of the van. She frowned and turned to the other side and acted annoyed. Everyone laughed looking at her. Gaurav again teased her, '*Okay, looks like somebody is a loser and has no courage to withstand a chocolate grab. I am the winner, let me have it,*' and he pulled the wrapper back to take a bite. Gayatri at once turned around, held his wrist and pulled Gaurav's hand towards her to take the bite.

Richa gave a loud applause, '*Yehhh... Lovely, bravo Gittu.*'

Gaurav was one of those romantic boyfriends who never let the romance vanish from a relationship that easy. He loved Gayatri a lot and he depended on these little moments for his happiness.

Gaurav took the next bite of the chocolate, after she had tasted it. Gayatri pulled the rest of it innocently and ate the chocolate alone.

Back in the hotel room 607, Amit and Ishita were sleeping one on top of the other. Ishita was lying down resting her head in Amit's arms and Amit grabbed her around in a cozy posture. They were tired after their long road driving. The next day was their anniversary which they wanted to celebrate among themselves only, without anyone's interference.

It was almost 2:00 p.m. in the afternoon, when their room bell rang. Once, twice, thrice.

'*Who is this bastard? Even after putting a do not disturb sign they are ringing the bell. I will complain about this.*' Amit uttered and shifted to the other side and slept.

Getting disturbed, Ishita rubbed her eyes and got up to check the door. As soon as she opened, she heard a young girl say, '*Can I have some water; the waiter is taking too long to bring it.*'

Looking at her condition, Ishita opened the door and let her in. She seemed to be a girl of around 15 or 16 years of age but was dressed in a glittery red off-shoulder dress; her chest seemed to be unnaturally heavy compared to her face and rest of the body. She looked tensed and in pain. Her lips were bleeding from one corner. Ishita got stunned looking at her and allowed her inside. She made her sit in the lounge area of the suite, and offered her water.

It looked like the girl was not aware of what she was doing. She looked terribly disturbed and fearful. Ishita sat beside her not knowing what to say. She noticed the sweat on her face. She was emanating the fragrance of a strong perfume. But she could feel that the girl was hurt on her face. The girl drank the whole glass of water but did not utter a word.

Ishita asked, '*Which room are you in?*' She did not reply and was just looking into the glass that she had emptied.

'*Do you want more water?*'

She nodded. Ishita poured in more water; the girl finished that too.

'*Do you want some more?*'

She denied.

'*What is your name?*'

There was another patch of silence.

Amit was fast asleep in the other room and did not hear the girls.

The girl looked around the room as if looking for a needle in a haystack.

There was a sofa at one corner, with a big window behind the curtains, which actually opened to a huge backyard. Hence there were heavy curtains that were always drawn. In front was a glass center table, sidewise along the walls were some decorative vases. The left side was the entrance of the room, the front was a corridor which was the way towards the washroom and further ahead was the door to the bedroom which was closed. On the right was a huge television and a wooden table where she saw that some luggage was kept.

The girl was in utter silence and did not speak a word. Ishita had to go to the loo and she said to the girl, 'Just wait a minute, I will be back from the washroom.' She rushed to the washroom.

When she returned, she could see no one in the room.

She looked for her in the room, and even her bedroom but she was nowhere. She opened the door to look outside if the girl had left. But she could not see her anywhere in the corridor. She came back to the room and sat on the sofa thinking about what just happened. She could see that the glass from which the girl drank the water was left with some blood strains which might be from the wound on her lips.

All of a sudden Ishita realised that the curtains were waving with the wind. She got up and removed the curtains and what she saw left her shocked with no bounds. The window was wide open, one look out of it and a scream choked her voice. The girl was lying in a pool of blood on the ground. Ishita's head swam and she felt dizzy. She was losing her grip. She held the vase placed next to the window but fell unconscious on the floor along with the vase. The sound of the breaking vase was loud enough to wake Amit up. He rushed outside the room calling her name. To his surprise, he saw Ishita lying unconscious on the floor and the vase shattered next to her. He ran to Ishita and sprinkled water on her face from the jug kept on the center table.

'*Ishita... Ishita... wake up! What happened?*' Amit called her, worried. He took her in his arms and made her lie on the sofa and called the reception for a doctor or some first aid.

'*Yes sir, we have an in-house doctor. I am just sending him.*' The receptionist said over the intercom.

Amit again sprinkled some water over Ishita and shook her by her shoulders to bring her back to consciousness. Ishita opened her eyes and started weeping, '*Amit, that girl jumped…she is lying on the ground.*' Ishita pointed her finger towards the window.

'*What?*' Amit rushed to the window and peeped down, but he could not see anything or anybody over there.

'*Where? There is no one on the ground. Where did you see?*'

Ishita got up flabbergasted. She looked down from the window but she could also not see anybody.

'She was there just now! I saw her in a pool of blood.'

Tears were rolling down her eyes as she narrated the story to him about how this girl had come to their suite and how this all had happened. She showed him the glass with blood stains. There was a knock at the door and in came a doctor with a housekeeping guy. The doctor came and examined her. Ishita narrated the story to the doctor as well and asked the boy to go and check downstairs in the back yard. The service boy along with the doctor and Amit went downstairs to look for that girl. Ishita was looking at them from the window while they were searching for any traces of the girl on the ground. The service boy looked above at Ishita and shook his hands and said, '*Ma'am, there is nothing down here.*' Ishita wanted to show him the glass, but the glass was also not there.

Amit and the doctor came back to the suite after the search.

'*Amit, there was a glass here from which she drank water. I had showed it to you, right?*' Ishita enquired as soon as she saw Amit.

'*Yeah, maybe the service boy took it.*' He called up the reception to enquire about that, but they said he did not pick any glass. Amit also got confused if he had actually seen that glass. Ishita was in total shock. She could not believe herself. She looked towards the window. Her head was spinning. She just gave up on everything and walked to the bedroom to take a nap. Amit thanked the doctor and closed the door behind him. He went inside the room to find Ishita half sitting on the bed, raised by two pillows. Her eyes were wide open as if something was running inside of her mind. Amit came and sat beside her. He lifted her face by her chin, '*Please look here.*' She was still in great shock. '*Please come out of it, leave it, and forget whatever it was. We have come here for our anniversary that's tomorrow. Please cheer up and... and... and...*' Amit came closer for a kiss that made her smile.

***

CHAPTER 13

THE BALLROOM

It was eight in the evening. The ballroom was well decorated with fairy lights and a DJ was standing in a corner behind his console. In front of him was an open large area. The bar was towards the opposite side with various kinds of glasses, mugs, shots, etc for various drinks. Some wine glasses were placed over the counter for quick pouring. Several bartenders were standing behind the wooden bar unit. On the other side, there was a sitting area with a long buffet hosting exotic cuisines from around the world. It had everything from Mexican, Thai, Japanese, Chinese and Indian. The area was huge and every table had a beautiful hand-made candle burning and a rose in a pretty small vase.

The clients in the hotel were all invited. A joyous and jubilant crowd was in.

The crowd present over there was of different types, some were with families and some with friends, some also with foreigners and there was also a huge gang of youngsters.

When Lavanya entered the room, she found it quite crowded. She looked around, but there was no one she saw who looked familiar. She was dressed in a normal denim capri and a deep red floral top. She went to one of the counters.

'Can I have one Sangria white wine please?'

The bartender nodded and prepared the same. Lavanya glanced around to look for someone known. But to be specific, her eyes were searching for Gayatri. She was the only familiar face she had found in the morning and was thinking if she would have been here, Lavanya would have had some company.

Her exotic fruity sangria was ready and was handed over to her. She took it up and then moved to the snacks corner to pick up a portion of peanut salad and then did she grab a corner seat from where the whole event was visible. She sat down and was browsing her phone to find some WhatsApp messages from her friends, from her dad and of course a few messages from Rachit, which she did not respond to.

'*Hey lovely! May I share the table with you?*' It was Gayatri in a beautiful black printed dress. She was looking very attractive in her simple makeup and loose curls and side-parted hair.

Lavanya beamed, '*Of course sweetheart, I was diligently looking for you. Where are your friends?*'

Gayatri pointed her finger and said, '*They are there at the bar.*'

Lavanya was intrigued, '*You don't take liquor?*'

Gayatri smiled, '*No ma'am, I don't take much. They will bring me a Breezer or Spritzer.*'

Once Gayatri had settled they started with the usual introductory conversation.

Lavanya asked, '*So, how was your day?*'

Gayatri replied, '*It was good, ma'am.*'

Lavanya interrupted, '*Call me Lavanya please.*'

Lavanya smiled and continued, '*So where do you belong to?*'

Gayatri answered, '*I have come here for a college excursion with my other college friends from Hyderabad. Basically I belong to Pune.*'

Richa, Gaurav, and Abhay also joined them with their plates of starters and drinks.

Lavanya asked, '*Gayatri, in the magazine it was mentioned about some extra senses and feeling that you experience, is it really true? I read your portion of the article and was curious about it.*'

It seemed like her question had given the occupants of the table an interesting pause. Everyone stopped whatever they were talking and doing and expectantly looked at Lavanya for a reply.

An embarrassed Lavanya uttered, '*Oh! Apologies if it's something personal.*'

Gayatri smiled and said, '*No no, it's fine Lavanya. In fact, I will tell all of you about my inner feelings and inner vision. Richa knows about it partly.*

Okay, let me start from my childhood.

'I was the only child of my parents. Both my parents had been working, Dad was into a government job and Mom had been a college lecturer. So there were times when I was all alone. I had only a few friends as I loved to keep myself occupied with books and paintings. I do remember when I was 11- 12 years old, I used to manage my school, studies, and home as well as helped Mom in the kitchen and other things. Initially, it started with seeing things in dreams which was how it was till now. I was 12 years old and was able to see some things in my dreams and later on, could find them happening in real. Initially, I was scared. I told my mom and dad and we went to many doctors. We visited psychiatrists and some Babas as well but nothing could cure me. There were days when I feared to sleep. Slowly, slowly, I started getting used to it.

Then one day, what I envisioned proved to be a real turning point in my life, which shattered my life. It was raining heavily; my mom and dad had gone to a nearby village for some office work. I was alone at home.

I went to the kitchen to get cook something for myself and accidentally, it seemed like I missed to turn the gas knob off. I came back in my room with my sandwiches and coffee and was about to switch on the lights, when suddenly the lights of my house went off. I was terrified and was trembling and then I saw my parents. They were back and that made me feel safe. I felt relaxed. I had my sandwiches and went to sleep.

The next morning when I woke up, there were a lot of people outside my home. My masi (maternal aunt) had been at the door for long and was ringing the doorbell.

I opened the door and my masi just rushed into the kitchen and switched off the gas and opened all windows and doors.

She hugged me hard.

Your mom called me up and asked me to see you and check your gas cylinder. She also told me to take care of you.

I was surprised as mom was back home yesterday night; then why would she call masi? I went back to check her room but she was not there and no signs of her being back.

I tried to call her on her cell phone and to our surprise, it was picked up by a policeman and it was him who told us that my parents had met with an accident while returning to Pune.

I was totally shattered. In that accident, I lost my mom and dad. It was them who saved me from the accident at home. They had turned the electricity off and had made a call to my masi to tell her to take care of me.

And do you know when we got her cell phone back; her last call was not to masi. We still don't know who called masi.

After that incident, I stayed with my masi and I still see those glimpses or you can say that some souls have been a part of my daily life now. Also, you might not like to believe but I had many such experiences. For you, these things might sound like out of a horror film like but all this truly happened with me.'

Everybody on the table was dumbstruck.

Gayatri continued -

'There is another incident that I wish to share.

A few months later, I met a lady in the park of my colony where I was playing. I did not know her. I was sitting on a bench in the park. She came and sat beside me. She started chatting and during the conversation I told her about my dreams.'

She smiled and added, 'Well till now I don't understand why I told her. But the conversation with her gave a direction to my dreams and made me come out of my insomnia and depression. She told me to use those dreams to save the world; she congratulated me for being privileged to have such a boon. I should thank God to be the privileged child who has been chosen for some noble cause. That touched me and later on, I started trying to save people whom I saw in my dreams. The dreams used to be good as well as bad. I started handling both of them nicely. Slowly and gradually, I started to see such glimpses during day time as well. I don't know when it would appear before me and sometimes, I don't even know how to resolve them. Sometimes they are a total mystery. Like since the time, I have entered this hotel, I am seeing some glimpses. I am not sure why it is and what I need to do for it. Is it a sign of danger or something just not right?

Gayatri paused, as she could see the glimpse again. This time it was a little clearer.

'That's interesting. What is it that you sensed?' Lavanya asked.

'I can see a figure of a young girl about 12-15 years of age, wearing a frock and her frock that has blood stains and there is a silhoute of three girls standing behind her. I can recognize one as myself and based on what I saw just now, it seems the second one is you, Lavanya and there is also a third lady with us, whom I can't recognize but she is definitely not Richa.'

'How can you be so confident it's me?' Lavanya asked surprised.

'Actually, until now I was unable to figure out the other two girls except me but today after meeting you, your today's dress and your movements, I am sure it is you.

Well, right now I am not sure what this relates to or what are we supposed to do.'

Looking at Gayatri getting into a trance, Richa paused and snapped her fingers before her eyes and said, *'Hey, little Miss Muffet,*

Sat on a tuffet,

Want to have your buffet?'

And everybody laughed out loud.

They continued with their talks and discussion about every-day life. Lavanya told everyone about Arshi and what an adorable little doll she is. She also talked about her business and asked Gayatri and her friends about their research papers.

It was around 10:00 p.m. at night. The crowd was in full swing. The dance floor was lighting in accordance with the foot taps. The disco lights flashed color on everyone's face and a majority of the crowd was busy dancing, wearing their beautiful masks which were being provided by the hotel staff right at the entrance of the hall.

Ishita and Amit entered the ball. It was the eve of their wedding anniversary. Both of them were happy about completing their one year of togetherness. Ishita was dressed like a doll, made-up and draped in a pink evening gown. Her hair were up in a bun decorated by designer pins. Amit was in his best tuxedo.

They were looking their best. As soon as they entered they caught the attention of everyone present in the room. Few of the people cleared the center of the floor for them and they took the dance floor with much grace and enjoyment.

The music was on and the DJ was playing tango and cha-cha-cha.

They both tapped to the beat and performed a perfect salsa with all the moves and lifts performed to a tee. Amit lifted Ishita up in his arms and swirled on the floor. With every move, their love for each other deepened. With every twist, the intimacy enhanced. With every lift, their trust for each other strengthened. They were so much in love and it showed.

Everybody on the floor was applauding and encouraging them.

They finished their performance with Ishita bending backwards on Amit's arm and looking lovingly into each other's eyes.

Gayatri captured their picture on her mobile. The whole room reverberated with claps and whistles. The hotel manager took the mic and announced to the crowd that the couple have their first wedding anniversary the coming day.

Ishita was introduced as the cover girl of the magazine and Gayatri's ears buzzed.

She could figure out Ishita being the third one in the vague visions she had been seeing ever since she had been in this hotel.

'*Lavanya, do you recognize her? She is the third lady on the cover page that we share.*' Gayatri said happily.

'*Oh, yes. You are right. What a coincidence! I could have never imagined that we will be meeting so soon like this.*'

And then, the host took over the mic and made another announcement.

'*Our hotel is privileged to have the all three cover girls of a leading magazine–The Women of Today with us today. Please give a loud applause for Gayatri and Lavanya as well. Gayatri and Lavanya, please come up on the stage.*'

They both walked to the center of the stage where Ishita was already present.

The crowd further applauded the trio.

The host continued, '*To introduce these ladies in a few words isn't justice to them. They are the real heroes of our society. Our hotel is proud to share a copy of the magazine with all of our clients to have a read about the ladies and their brave stories.*'

The crowd cheered loudly.

Meanwhile, the three of them held hand in hand and bowed to the crowd.

They hugged each other and wished for each other's goodwill. Few people came forward to congratulate them.

Amit escorted the ladies to a table to give them time to know each other. He himself left for the bar counter.

Ishita was very happy to meet the others. They talked about coincidence, God's will and something which was supernatural that had brought the three unknowns together and was thanking the editor who had featured them together. They spent the rest of the time discussing their lives, home, and work. All the three ladies gelled really well.

It was half-past one now. They had already celebrated and cut the anniversary cake of Ishita and Amit and had had a good time with the group of strangers who had become known soon. The hotel staff had organized for a three-tier red velvet cake which was made available for the huge gathering. Everyone congratulated the young couple and praised them for their looks.

The party was soon over.

They came out of the party hall and waved each other a goodnight and left for their rooms. Gayatri picked up the magazine before leaving for her room.

She was walking beside Richa when suddenly she saw the same girl she had seen in the morning while leaving for the seminar. Her dress was eye-catching. She was dressed way too maturely and was wearing a loud makeup. She was nervy and her face could describe her innocence. As Gayatri walked through she could not take her eyes off her. Gayatri could see some pain in the girls' eyes. She could sense that there was something that this girl was hiding; there was a mystery around her.

Gayatri did not say anything; she just passed through the corridor to her door.

Lavanya was also swiping her key card when she saw a beautiful girl dressed in loud off-shoulder dress and pointed heels passing by her along with a hotel boy.

Lavanya stopped to greet her, '*Hey, you look awesome! Where are you roaming alone at this time?*'

The girl turned around but kept walking without replying to the question. Lavanya was a bit surprised but she went inside her room as she was very sleepy.

CHAPTER 14

THE MAGAZINE

Gayatri was in her room and had changed into her night suit but her head was besieged by the thoughts of that little girl.

Richa took to bed and was soon snoring.

Gayatri layed down but was unable to close her eyes. She turned to her side and her hand touched the magazine. She took the magazine, gazed at the cover page for a few moments and then sat up and started flipping the pages.

She kept turning over and suddenly her eyes paused on a picture. It was a similar picture of a girl in a frock and blood spilled around her. She jumped out of her skin! It was the same image she was seeing until now. The heading of the page read '*Human Trafficking*'.

Her eyes stoned and her ears were blocked. She could not speak either. She gathered herself to pour a glass of water for herself. She now understood that this is what she needs to read now. She got up and sat against a pillow. She stretched her legs and she placed another pillow on her lap and started reading the article.

It contained information and awareness about human trafficking.

What is Human Trafficking and what are its types?

It talked about Human Trafficking being the fastest growing criminal business because of its very high-profit potential. It mentioned that unlike any other business, under Human Trafficking a human can be sold many numbers of times and can be utilized on multiple occasions.

It is a business that is considered to be second largest after the drug trafficking in terms of profitability.

It not only includes sex rackets but also organ stealing, bonded slavery, forced labour, debt bondage, forced marriage, and many other forms.

It has been estimated that a count ranging from 4 to 24 million of people have been stuck or victimized in such trafficking. But the stats can be questioned as United Nations quote that the stats can be disruptive due to the hidden nature of the work process and lack of systematic reporting. Hence, it can be considered much more than the estimated count. Also, the estimated profit was being considered more than $32 billion annually, worldwide.

The victims are mostly young adults between the age group 18-25 years. It was highlighted in bold that these days young children of the age group 10-15 years are the top victims. An estimation of 1.2 million children are trafficked for either sexual exploitation or dumped into brothels or are put into bonded labour.

There are many middlemen also known as Pimps and Johns who protect the secrecy of the business and are the most profited owners. The Johns can earn 20 times of what they paid for buying the victim. 90% of the victims are females who are often exploited sexually.

It then talked about how they were conditioned and threatened, most of them are either threatened in the name of their family members or fear of death or physical abuse or beating, confinement, starvation, money, forced drugs, rape and gang brutality to name a few.

The victims are fulminated and terrorized to the extent that they become helpless and give in to submission.

The article also talked about how they got into such

situations. This information was far more annoying, disturbing and mind-boggling.

It had examples of a few cases, one of which said that there was a girl who had been sold by her own father, then another of a boyfriend selling his girlfriend, a neighbour kidnapping a little girl, a little boy been picked up from school and many more. The victims were parcelled or exported to other countries and then their passports were seized so that they could never return to their home. This was a curse not only in India but had been spreading like a virus in the whole world.

These Johns could be anybody from a known person to some stranger. You can never know if you are really in a safe company.

Gayatri got so absorbed in the magazine that she lost the track of time. It was almost dawn; she was awake the whole night. She kept on reading every single line and felt the trauma the victims would have gone through. She paused and wondered about their lives, the pain so many of them would have gone through, the pain of their families. She even felt terrified thinking about the prospects of human trafficking.

Then next were the symptoms that any common man can identify. These victims could have been roaming in your city and they could be so helpless to gather the courage to ask for help or dare to run away.

They could be some lonely girls, who avoid eye contact. Fear and pain could be seen on their faces and eyes. They might have some bruises or cuts at unusual places. They would speak less. They might be wearing some odd dresses misfit for their age.

If anybody finds such girls or women, he or she should come up and join hands against such crime. We the citizens must stand against these crimes. Any citizen who falls into such a fishy situation or has found some ambiguity happening in their vicinity, they should follow some basic pointers and run through a questionnaire with the suspected person.

1. How did she come here?

2. Is anybody threatening her or is her family in danger?

3. Did anybody give her any pain?

4. Does she need help?

5. Does her family need help?

6. Is she getting paid for her work?

And so on.

At the end of the article, there were some helpline numbers mentioned, and the numbers of Delhi commission of women's cell was also provided.

Gayatri got absorbed in this and started linking her glimpse with the article and the two girls whom she saw in the last two days. She felt like she was here for a big cause and might need help from Lavanya and Ishita since she saw both of them in her vision.

It was almost 7:00 in the morning. She got up and rang the intercom number of Lavanya and asked her to reach the breakfast table by 8:00. Next she called Ishita and asked her for the same thing.

It was Ishita's anniversary. She was a little reluctant initially but when Gayatri insisted and mentioned that it was something urgent and requested her to be there for just 30 minutes, she agreed.

Now it was time for Gayatri to act. She rushed to the washroom to take a shower and got ready. She reached the restaurant first and took a corner table. She was carrying two copies of the magazine with her to show to Lavanya and Ishita.

Ishita reached next. Gayatri waved at her and she walked directly to her. By that time Lavanya also came.

All three settled themselves on a corner round table.

Gayatri opened the magazine to the article on Human

Trafficking and handed it over to both of them.

'Girls, I would just take 10 minutes of your time and would request your consent for the same. But of course, I am granting you twelve hours to think about it and respond.' Both of them carried a curious look on their faces.

Gayatri continued, '*Please read this article, I am pretty sure something fishy like this is happening here.*'

Lavanya took a glance at the heading and exclaimed, '*What nonsense?*'

Gayatri quickly came to her defence and said, '*I can sense it but l am right now not totally sure as I don't have any evidence to back my statement.*'

Lavanya was reading the article. Without lifting her eyes, she asked, '*What do you want from me?*'

Gayatri replied, '*I just wanted to ask you guys to help me out in this cause. I know, I am here for some really good cause and for now I can comprehend to some extent that you guys are here to supplement me. Till now the things I have envisioned, were within my courage and range to accomplish. But this time, without both of you this project is not going to be completed. I need your consent and help in planning out a target for this project.*'

Till now Ishita was silent and was just listening. She was able to connect to that girl who had come to her room. She had not yet disclosed that incident to these girls. She was in a shock as she connected the dots and was trying to digest the words of Gayatri.

Lavanya wasn't convinced. She blurted, '*Lady, I just met you yesterday. I have listened about your sixth sense and all that stuff, this doesn't mean I would start listening to you and just keep following you on whatever you say. Sorry man, It's not my cup of tea.*'

She lifted her hands up in the air and brought them down with a thud on the table and said, '*You called me here. I came and listened to you. So now that I have heard you, can I take your leave?*'

Ishita held Lavanya's hand, 'Please, one second. If you have listened so much, can you please spare five more minutes? I want to share something.'

Lavanya was irritated, '*Now what?*'

Ishita pleaded, '*Please sit down. Trust me, it won't take more than 5 minutes.*'

Lavanya leaned back on her chair.

Ishita narrated the whole story in short within 5 minutes about the girl who knocked at her room and then disappeared.

Ishita said, '*Gayatri, I am with you, as that event is not wiping off my mind. I can now relate to it and even I think that something fishy is happening here. Lavanya, we need to sit together and come up with some plan to crack this mystery. There must be some reason behind this coincidence of our meeting. The three of us on the cover page and the three of us now sitting here and talking about the same topic. Lavanya, please understand we would be incomplete without you. Our trio has to be one. Please say yes*'.

Ishita placed her hand over Lavanya's.

Lavanya pulled her hand out and said, '*I have my meeting at Connaught Place. I have to reach there before 10 a.m. Can I take your leave now?*'

Gayatri and Ishita slumped and just nodded. Lavanya got up and walked off.

Gayatri called after her as she was walking out, '*Please think about it once again.*'

Both of them kept quiet for some time. They were completely blank as they were not able to make out what to do and how to do.

Ishita's phone rang, it was Amit.

She took the call, '*Yeah I came downstairs. Yes, please come down to the restaurant for breakfast.*'

CHAPTER 15

LAVANYA'S CONSENT

The clock was showing 3:00 a.m. The hotel Lalita Palace was sunk into a stony silence. All hoteliers were in their rooms. The cleaning and housekeeping staff were onto their work, completing their shifts.

Lavanya was still awake in her room. She was reading something. She had almost forgotten the discussion that had happened over breakfast with Ishita and Gayatri.

Her room was lit dim. She just had the bedside lamps on to read.

She was lying on her bed and relaxing. Suddenly a sequence of car lights flashed from her window, lighting the curtains drwan across the window in the front.

She didn't pay much heed to it but then she heard some noises which were more of stressed whispers. Again, more car lights brought dashes of light into her room.

She blabbered, '*These fucking guys don't have any other time to make all this noise and flash lights.*'

She wanted to check who it was who was disturbing her peace. She got up from her bed and went to the window. She could see some commotion under her window.

She looked at it for a few minutes, then turned around to get back in bed, From the corner of her eye she caught the movement of some girls in glittery frocks who looked to be not more than 8–10 years old.

Lavanya withdrew the curtains a little to look more clearly, but the movement was so swift and quick that she could not see the girls again. To add to her misery the trees, plants and the boundary wall, everything was blocking her view.

She tried hard to look through...

She heard the sound of music... it was her phone ringing.

She ran at once to check and to her surprise, it was '*Mom calling*' with a picture of mom lighting up the screen.

'*Mom... at this time*!' Lavanya murmured and picked up the call.

'*Mom... what happened? Calling at this time...Is everything fine at home? Arshi...Is she fine?*'

The voice of her Mom boomed through the phone, '*Are... Puttar, thand rakh... sab vadiya ha itthe...*'

Lavanya was irritated. '*Then why are you calling at this hour?*'

Her Mom sounded almost in tears when she said, '*Mainu twadi vadi fikr ho rahi si.*'

Lavanya was further irritated, '*What, mom... pleases, not at this time...*'

Her Mom didn't pay attention to her and continued, '*Mrs Khanna mainu puch rahi si, vihah de vaste, par saanu ki... mainu kismat da siyappa.*

Palle nai dhela, kardi mela mela...fitteh munh!!'

Lavanya could take this no more, '*Mom, please don't start again now. It's very late. Go to sleep now.*'

Her dejected Mom said, 'Chalo ji, *Rab Rakhan.*'

Lavanya was feeling as dejected. She said a quick, '*Good night, Mom. Bye,*' and hung up.

Lavanya went back to check the outside but everything had just vanished.

She came back to her bed after trying to see if she can

find anything and was fast asleep.

She was hardly asleep for 30 mins when she woke up screaming.

She was dripping with sweat, although the air conditioner in the room was working fine.

She immediately took to the intercom.

'Hello... Gayatri, I am in with you girls. See you at breakfast.'

CHAPTER 16

GIRLS GANG

It was the same breakfast table that the GIRL GANG [Gayatri, Ishita, Richa and Lavanya] had occupied the last time.

Gayatri began, '*Lavanya, if you can share your reason for accepting our proposal*, it might help us.'

Lavanya held her head and replied, '*Last night I saw some movement from the back window of my room; it was dark so I couldn't see clearly and the trees and other things blocked my view but something was going on there. And then when I slept, I saw my daughter getting trapped in such a situation like the one we read about in the magazine which brought me back to my senses. Now, if I don't help you guys. I won't be able to live in peace.*'

She placed her palm over Gayatri's.

Ishita took control of the flowing emotions and said, '*Ok Girls, we now need a code word to alert each other whenever someone is in trouble, now that we are all in this all together.*'

Lavanya smiled and blurted, '***TAKT***'

'*What's that!?*' The others echoed.

Lavanya said, '*It's my motto for whomsoever would cause any trouble in my life–Teri Aisi Ki Taisi.*'

'*Wow...!*' Said everyone together.

Ishita added, '*Now actually we have to be very careful. We don't know how it is going to happen and how we are going to crack it. We have to plan and follow accordingly.'*

Ishita pulled up a tissue paper from the stand and started scribbling.

Ishita said, *'For how many days more are you guys in this hotel?'*

Gayatri said, '*2 days.*'

Ishita said, '*1.*'

Richa said, '*2 days*'

Lavanya said, '*One. My checkout is tomorrow.*'

Ishita said what everyone was thinking, '*So first of all, we need to extend our stay for at least 5 days. But we need to do it very carefully.*'

Gayatri added, '*Richa, my friends and I can easily extend our stay as our event has got postoned. We had to extend anyway.*'

Ishita, who had been thinking about what she can do, said, '*I can bring up some medical issues and get my stay extended as well. But yes, I will have to convince my husband.*'

Lavanya's phone rang, but she disconnected.

Ishita said, '*You can take your call.*'

'*It's okay.*'

The phone rang again; she picked up to answer and blurted, '*Anything urgent, Rachit?*'

She heard him and disconnected.

Everyone was looking at Lavanya's eyes and waiting for her to tell them on her own what had just happened.

Lavanya looked at their faces and said, '*Nothing girls... My boyfriend...*'

Gayatri smiled, '*Ohhh...*'

Lavanya rolled her eyes and said, '*And he is coming here this evening.*'

Ishita's smile widened, '*Wow good! You have the perfect reason to extend your holidays. And, we have an additional team member.'*

Ishita grabbed the reins of the conversation and said, '*So far so good; we all have a good reason now. We would do a 5D plan now.*

Day 1–Just monitoring.

Day 2–Monitoring Questioning

Day 3–Relating and connecting

Day 4–Execution

Day 5 – Action Plan

'*From now on, we will communicate through our cell phones. No use of intercoms. I am creating a WhatsApp group and will add you all and most importantly, we will try to maximize the use of smilies and icons to convey what we see/feel/hear. No text messages.'*

Lavanya was confused, '*How exactly?'*

Ishita explained, '*Like if you want to meet, send a coffee cup icon, if you want to say or share something use the open mouth icon, if you want to call, use a telephone icon.'*

Richa was impressed, '*Incredible! That's an amazing idea, Ishita.'*

Ishita said, '*Wherever anyone finds something mysterious or fishy, take a picture of it and post it in the group. Now everyone has to save those pictures on Google drive and then delete it from Whatsapp. So that in case we lose our phone, nobody can figure out what were we doing.'*

Lavanya was listening intently, 'Yes, that should work.'

Ishita added, *'And after this we would not be meeting all together like this. We would only be meeting in pairs of two. Rest we would talk in a conference call at night from our rooms.'*

Ishita smiled and boomed, '*So commandos, any questions?'*

Lavanya had one. '*Do you think it would be this easy that we would be able to resolve some big case in like 5 days? Just like that and boom!'*

Ishita explained her point. '*No Lavanya, I don't think so, because as far as I know, these gangs are usually highly linked and work at a very high level and in total secrecy. We might not be able to catch them or may not even be able to get any clue. Looking into such activities happening in this popular five-star hotel doesn't seem to be an easy one. I am really afraid too.*'

Gayatri added, '*All we can do is try and try we will.*'

Ishita nodded but said, '*And yes, personal safety is foremost. We have to save ourselves and each other first then only we would be able to save others.*'

Everyone nodded and shook hands to that. A sense of satisfaction could be seen on everyone's face. Also, a moment of self-glorification was fairly visible too. They had a plan and they were going to indulge in something which they had never thought of doing or ever dreamt of. They were scared but determined.

The girl gang hugged each other and wished each other good luck before parting ways.

They dispersed and left for their agendas for the day with a promise to follow up on the plan and stay connected as and when required and update each other about their safety.

CHAPTER 17

LOVE IS IN THE AIR

Lavanya's room, evening at 7:00 p.m.

Rachit had reached the hotel by 5:30 p.m. and had met Lavanya. They were in her room. The first thing Lavanya asked when he came was, *'How is Arshi?'* To which Rachit patiently replied that she was fine and that bhabhi was taking extra care of her along with Lavanya's father. She was eating her food in time and is happy. She did ask everyday about Lavnaya and when would she come back, but everyone convinced her of Lavanya's early return.

Lavanya was happy to hear that Arshi was fine and missed her mother. She just couldn't wait to go back and hug her child. She had not been away from her daughter for this long ever and there were 5 more days to go, but it was that dream about Arshi being trapped that made her stay here for this cause. Being a mother she wanted her daughter to live in a safe world and this was the least she could do.

After talking casually for a bit, they ordered tea and vegetable pakodas from room service.

'Lavanya, if you are uncomfortable, I can get a separate room. I am okay with anything.' Rachit said softly, fearing that Lavanya might get offended.

He had actually come down to spend some quality time with Lavanya so that he could apologize to her and tell her that he loved her and could not live without her. He also wanted to sort out all the issues between them.

'No, that's fine Rachit. We can share the room and bed. I trust you.' She smiled.

Lavanya also felt a little content knowing that Rachit was with her in this moment. In her heart, she loved him, but her ethos did not allow her to confess the same.

Lavanya was wearing a casual legging and a georgette printed top which was her usual nightwear. Rachit freshened up and was in his t-shirt and boxers. They looked extremely comfortable in each other's presence.

The room service guy came and placed the tea and pakodas for them on the table, which they both rejoiced.

Lavanya climbed on the bed and couched under the duvet and said, *'Rachit, please make tea and pass on the pakodas to me please.'*

'Anything for you, ma'am.', Rachit smiled and bowed before her.

They both laughed aloud and Rachit jumped on the bed and cuddled up with Lavanya.

He lovingly looked at Lavanya and smiled. Lavanya felt a little shy but smiled back. They came closer and enveloped in a passionate kiss which lasted for long. Rachit removed Lavanya's hair away from her face and gazed into her deep set eyes. He was so in love with her and so was Lavanya. Having known each other for such a long time, both of them had not only loved each other unconditionally but also shared a relationship of deep respect.

It had been long Lavanya had felt such contentment which made her forget everything except that she was in Rachit's arms.

***

Ishita's room, evening at 7:00 p.m.

'I am going to take a shower.'

'Ok, dear!' Ishita gave a smirk and engrossed herself back

into her book.

'*Why are you smiling like this? Hope you aren't plotting any prank; else I am going to cuddle you tight and not let go.*' Amit gestured by hugging himself tight.

'*No darling, nothing. I have changed now.*'

Amit raised an eyebrow in disbelief and locked himself in the restroom.

Ishita was counting down…10–9–8 – 7… and there came a scream from the bathroom!

'*Ishitaaaaa, I am gonna kill you!!*'

Ishita couldn't stop her laughter. She clutched her stomach laughing and fell headfirst on the pillow next to her, while Amit opened the door.

Ishita had hid lots of dry mud in the folded bath towels. After shower as Amit lifted the towel off the overhead stand to wipe himself, he was drenched in mud from head to toe.

Amit kept standing there like a naughty child who had just slipped himself into a pool of mud.

Ishita kept laughing holding her stomach.

Amit looked at his sexy wife and her pranks made her sexier to him. He came next to her and dragged her to the washroom and confined her in his grip.

'*You made me dirty and now we will clean all this up together.*'

He pulled her into the shower and kissed her on her lips softly.

They both engrossed in a passionate love making under the shower.

***

Gayatri's room, evening at 7:00 p.m.

All the four friends were just back from their conference. They all were sitting down in Gayatri's room.

Richa said she was hungry and held Abhay's hand to take him to the restaurant downstairs.

'*Do you want anything to eat, Gayatri?*' Richa checked before leaving.

'*Nothing darling!*'

Gayatri and Gaurav were now left alone in the room. Gaurav was sitting on the chair next to the bed where Gayatri was sitting, tired after the long day's work.

After they left, there was a pin-drop silence in the room.

They were not looking at each other.

After 5 minutes of silence, Gayatri broke it and said, '*Would you mind if I go and freshen up in a few minutes?*'

Gaurav said, '*Not an issue.*'

Gayatri suggested, '*You can watch the television till then.*'

Gaurav switched on the TV and was browsing the channels.

Gayatri was back in a few minutes, in a baby pink night suit with teddy bear print. She looked absolutely adorable in that outfit.

Gaurav's eyes got glued on her face.

There was a song playing on the TV from the movie *Hum dil de chuke sanam*—

Aankhon ki kustakhiyan maaf ho.......

Gayatri could feel a strong tingle in her stomach with the way Gaurav was gazing her. The want was clearly written on his face.

'*What Gaurav?*' She softly asked with a smile.

Gaurav shook his head and went back to his TV.

As he changed the channel, the other channel had *Pehla Nasha* playing with Amir Khan floating his sweater in the air.

Their hearts were beating with every beat of the song.

'*Can you pass me the glass of water please?*' Gayatri interrupted.

Gaurav lifted the glass and gave it to her. Their hands touched during the exchange and an electric current surged threw both of them and the glass fell before one cold hand it over and other could hold it.

Gaurav was quick to say, '*I am sorry. My bad.*'

Gayatri was next, '*I am sorry too.*'

They both bent down together to gather the pieces and their heads banged.

'*Ouch...*'

'*Ouch...*'

Gaurav took the lead, '*Let me pick it up. You please sit.*'

Gaurav collected the pieces. A more melodious background score was running from one of Arijit Singh hits, *Suno na sangmarmar*. Meanwhile, Gayatri had dialled the room service for cleaning up.

The TV songs were adding more charm to the whole situation. Songs have always been a medium to express love. They play a major role in young love stories adding more fuel to the romance and the situation and you feel every lyric suit you.

While Gaurav was removing the glass pieces to one side, one of the shards dug into his finger and a gush of blood flowed out of his hand.

'*Oh my God! You have got hurt. Leave it. I told you to let me do this.*' Gayatri jumped and held his hand and pulled him up to sit beside her.

She settled him and ran to grab the first-aid box.

She then sat beside Gaurav and kept grumbling about the wound. She seemed worried and concerned. Gaurav was just gazing at her face with eternal pleasure and was thanking the shard of glass for making this happen.

Gayatri was saying, '*Hope the Dettol is not hurting you.*'

Just a nod was the answer from a dumbstruck Gaurav. He felt like covering her face with kisses.

Gaurav asked suddenly, '*Can I kiss you?*'

Gayatri stopped doing whatever she was doing.

'*Can I kiss you?*' Gaurav's eyes were oozing with desire.

'*Why?*'

'*I don't know, but I want to.*'

He paused for a moment and then comforted her, '*You have the option to say no and I will leave the room at once.*'

Gayatri got numb.

'*Can I kiss you?*' Gaurav came closer and whispered.

Gayatri just closed her eyes in a moment.

Gaurav held Gayatri and kissed her slowly, gently, softly.

Although their intimate moment got obstructed within seconds by the sound of Richa and Abhay coming in from the restaurant.

In the next few hours, love was in the air in these three rooms. Post this, the three rooms elapsed into a convincing session. Lavanya was trying to convince Rachit about the Girls Gang's plan and about Arshi being with them for life.

Ishita was trying to convince Amit for being her support while she deals with the notorious deeds going on in the hotel.

And Gayatri and Richa were convincing the boys about the plan and seeking their agreement for the same.

The 5 Ws (Who, Why, When, Where, & What) were echoed in every next line. A series of explanations and courageous appearances were being showcased. All the girls were trying hard to loop in people they loved and trusted to be a part of this. They needed more strength and support to make this plan work.

After much persistance did their phones got buzzed with notifications carrying smilies from all the ladies in the Girls Gang Whatsapp group. Finally the first step of convincing was over successfully.

***

CHAPTER 18

DAY ONE

Amit and Ishita were sitting on the bedside couch. The clock was ticking to 8 in the morning. The beautiful yellow rays of sun were striking on the shining circular glass tea table through the glass window. Amit was as usual was reading the newspaper while sipping his tea.

Ishita was sliding her fingers over her phone and smiling to herself looking at some videos and messages.

These smartphones sometimes can certainly turn you into a clown.

The message alerts on Ishita's phone made Amit lift his eyes to look at Ishita. From her facial expression, he could guess it was something interesting.

'*Who's it?*' Amit raised his eyebrows.

Ishita read, '*Today is day 1. It is just the monitoring day. There are messages in the group that we have to be vigilant and keep our eyes open wherever we are. Also, there is a piece of information that there is again a ball dance scheduled today evening.*'

Amit had by now understood his wife and her pranks.

Amit asked, '*So what's for me today?*'

Ishita replied, '*We would take a round of the hotel and its special attractions today.*'

Ishita jumped up with a naughty smile and came and sat

on Amit's lap to give him a deep kiss. Her happiness knew no bounds when she found a positive response from Amit.

Ishita moved her face back and asked, '*So, my dear hubby, let's get ready and do some real action.*' She held him close and kissed him once again.

Amit picked her up and took her straight to the bathroom where they showered together and were soon dressed, Amit, in cool casuals with a red t-shirt and cargos and Ishita in a casual floral print maroon chiffon dress. They both looked very much like the true lovebirds that they were. They roamed around in the corridors as if wallowing in the luxury of the hotel.

The hotel had seven floors in total and about thirty rooms on each floor.

'*What do you say, from where should we start from?*' Ishita murmured.

Amit replied, '*Let's go to the reception and check out.*'

'*How can I help you Sir and Ma'am?*' The receptionist greeted.

Amit handled the situation, '*We wish to relax today. Could you suggest something interesting for us?*'

Receptionist was happy to help. '*Yes sure, why don't you try out our exotic spa, the basic panchkarma massage is being offered at 40% discount for our guests.*' She pulled out a brochure and explained to them the various packages.

'*This is great.*' Ishita agreed and they both were escorted towards the Spa.

It was on the 4th floor and in the extreme corner- to reach there, they had to pass through the whole corridor. As they were about to reach there, they saw two guards standing in front of the door.

Ishita slipped ahead and posed, '*Honey, please take a picture of mine!*'

They wanted to portray that they were just tourists

and were just roaming around in the hotel so that nobody questions them.

Amit was about to click, but one of the guards interrupted them. *'You can't take pictures here. It's not allowed.'*

Ishita pleaded in her baby sweet voice and convinced them for one click. The guards smiled at her eagerness and allowed them one click.

The entry to the Spa was beautiful through a huge wooden teak door that said *Spa*. Right inside the gate came the Spa reception where two women greeted both Ishita and Amit. The aroma of the whole area was very soothing, and there was some light classical music playing in the background. Two huge wooden seats were arranged across the reception area with a center table that had water and rose petals in a small bowl. Two clean hand towels were also carefully folded and kept in a handmade basket along with wet wipes. There was a bottle of bisleri and two glasses kept upside down. The receptionist asked both of them to wait while they prepare the Spa room.

Ishita and Amit both noticed the huge Buddha painting in the background and were mesmerized by the details.

There were separate sections for men and women. Amit and Ishita went into to their respective ones. They were given changing gowns.

A little girl of about 16 years of age entered the room with a bowl of oil and guided Ishita into a dimly lit room. It had a wooden bed and a washing chamber beside it for a steam bath. Various oils and massage creams were decorated on the top shelf of the wooden table. The music that reverberated from the outside

She asked Ishita to take off her clothes and relax on the wooden bed.

Initially, Ishita hesitated; then the girl made her sit on a wooden stool and started giving her a shoulder massage. It was so relaxing that Ishita got completely entranced. Then the girl slowly stripped off her undergarments and made her relax on the wooden bed.

Ishita and her body got completely relaxed during the massage, but suddenly, Ishita got alarmed and she started getting goosebumps. The relaxing massage was slowly getting converted into an erotic and sensual massage. The girl was touching her private parts inappropriately.

An alarmed Ishita shouted, '*Hey! Stop!*'

She sat up and quickly covered herself with a towel and asked, '*What are you doing?*'

The girl was embarrased, '*Sorry ma'am, are you not interested in an erotic massage?*'

'No! *Who told you to do this?*' Ishita said loudly.

The girl begged pardon, '*Sorry, ma'am, usually people come for that. I forgot to check the register. Please don't complain about me outside, else I would lose money.*'

The girl started pleading before Ishita with folded hands. Ishita took long breaths and calmed down. She talked to the girl.

'*What is your name?*'

'*Pinky*'

'*Pinky, are we visible in some camera or audio?*'

'*Ma'am, I am not sure, but we might be. Didi sometimes scolds some of us based on our performance, so I suppose she is able to see us. There might be a hidden CCTV camera somewhere.*'

'*Are you supposed to go to the men's area as well?*'

She was quiet.

'*Pinky, please tell me, are you doing this work of your own will or you are forced to do it?*'

She was quiet again.

'*Ma'am, your massage is over, and your steam bath is ready. Another girl will come to wipe you up after 15 minutes of steam bath.*'

'Pinky, I will come tomorrow and I want you to give me a massage. Same time.'

'You need to tell Didi for that.'

Ishita nodded and sat in the steam chamber.

Meanwhile, a furious Gayatri went to the reception and burst out;

'What the hell is this? This is your five-star hotel? Where is *my dress!'*

Gayatri's dress had gotten misplaced. She had sent it for ironing and had later got the reply that they don't have it with them anymore.

She was angry and was not going to tolerate such behaviour.

Receptionist beseeched, *'Ma'am, I am sorry. I will just check the laundry section.'*

The receptionist called the laundry executive and he came there within 7 minutes. Till then Gayatri was scolding and shouting at the staff. The laundry executive enquired for the description of her dress and assured her to bring it up in the next 2 hours.

Gayatri, *'No, I will go there myself and check.'*

Executive was scared now. *'We would bring it to you. Please give us a few hours, you don't have to worry, ma'am.'*

But Gayatri was stuck on her words; the helpless man had to take her to the laundry. It was in the upper basement and she accompanied him. Richa was also with her. They were initially asked to wait at the entrance. But Gayatri forced herself inside and insisted upon being showen how well they were searching for her dress.

The moment she entered, she felt like she had been here before. She knew the place. There were racks and ally of cupboards, cloth piles, and stacked sheets. There were chambers and big boilers at the far corner. She got guided through the sections of cupboards to the backside. She could see a few workers discussing about some sheet counts and segregating them.

Her eyes could not believe when she saw some red-stained sheets piled up at one side and others on the other side.

Gayatri was curious. '*Richa, are those bloodstains?*'

Richa was numb and could not utter a word.

The executive tapped Gayatri on the back, '*What are you doing here, ma'am?*'

He was carrying a dress, '*Is this the one ma'am?*'

Gayatri and Richa took the dress and left the laundry room and went straight back to their room. They could not believe what their eyes had just seen. Both of them were horrified by the sight of what they had seen. Those white sheets certainly had blood stains, or maybe period stains. Any girl could easily identify them even from a distance.

Lavanya and Rachit were in the hotel garden. The hotel had a beautiful lawn around its boundary wall. The hotel had an aesthetic architectural design and was necklaced with a narrow water channel, followed with an exotic flower garden with walking track around.

Lavanya was trying to map the out gate where she had seen the commotion a few days back. They both were walking hand in hand so that no one could guess that they were looking for cues. They looked so occupied amongst themselves that any passerby could have deciphered them as lovers.

Meanwhile, they were clicking some pictures, selfies, and sceneries.

'*Ma'am, you cannot take pictures here. It's a prohibited area. But you can take pictures at the front lawn of the hotel.*' One of the guards approached Lavanya to stop her from taking pictures.

Lavanya was surprised, '*Why? Is there any issue here?*'

'*It's a hotel rule.*' The guard pointed towards a signboard in a corner which said -

Photography is prohibited.

Rachit looked at Lavanya and shook his head to indicate not to click any more pictures.

Lavanya was trying to memorize the location. But she could not see anything out of the blue. She then checked with the guards if they can sit there for some time as that place was serene and quiet and they wished to spend some time in solitude.

When the guard agreed, both of them sat down on the garden seats trying to figure out if anything was unusual.

'*Love-girl, can you figure out something? It seems like there is a gate behind that thick bush.*' Rachit raised his eyebrow in the direction to guide Lavanya towards a corner bush at the boundary.

Lavanya tried to see where he was pointing out without making it obvious for the guards. She could recognize the same gate to be the same as she had seen from her room window.

'*Should we go and check that gate?*' Lavanya was about to make a get up.

'*Stop!*' Rachit pulled her back and she fell on his lap. She was in his arms. He bent over her face to kiss her.

'*Has the roadside guard turned back?*' Rachit whispered in her ears.

Lavanya squinted, '*Yes, they seemed to be coming towards us but have now turned back.*'

'*Maintain the position.*'

'*Okay.*'

The roadside guards made some signs to those guards at the gate as if they were told to keep an eye on Lavanya and Rachit and get them to leave the place. The guards at the gate strongly hit their wooden stick on the ground to make enough sound that can interrupt the privacy of Lavanya and Rachit.

Finally, they got up and left the place.

Ishita meanwhile shared the pictures of the spa entrance in their watsapp group.

Gayatri jumped up to see the same security guard uniform as those at the entrance of the laundry. Then there was another update from Lavanya which too showed the guards with the same kind of uniform. Interestingly, they were not the uniforms of the usual security guards of the hotel. But how come these guards had separate uniforms? Were they hired from some other agency?

***

CHAPTER 19

DAY TWO

'The spa was interesting; I am going for spa today again.'

The message from Ishita beeped in the Whatsapp group. After some time, a post from Lavanya stated she did some technical searches and found the logo on the uniforms of the security guards somewhat matched with five security providing companies and she was planning to visit them all.

Gayatri dropped the emoji of a '*happy person raising a hand*' to show her consent for accompanying her. Lavanya and Gayatri decided to meet outside of the hotel and take an auto to all of the agencies.

It was around 11:00 in the morning and Day 2 had already started. The heartbeat was high of all the three ladies. A sense of fear, palpitation, nervousness, anxiety and motivated courage was traversing through their veins. They needed to interpret the clues they had found yesterday and do something about it; they had to dig in deeper to find what actually was going on.

Gayatri was in her jeans and t-shirt and was waving towards the auto. Lavanya had been crossing the road in her Nike shoes, wearing white T and brown jeans. Both of them got into an auto.

Lavanya ordered, '*Bhaiya, Karol Bagh Chalo.*' *(Bhaiya, take us Karol Bagh.)*

Lavanya handed over the sheet to Gayatri which had the

five addresses. There were two from Karol Bagh, one from Faridabad, one from Vasant Kunj and one from Gurugram.

The Faridabad address was of *One Shot Securities, shop no 214, No 1 Market, Sector 1 Faridabad.*'

It had the tag line which said for all kind of security provider for homes, offices, clubs, bars, hotels, societies and personal bodyguards.

Gayatri said, '*Does this kind of punch line exist for all other security agencies?*'

Lavanya took the sheet from her and said, '*Let me see.*' She pulled the sheet to read between the lines.

Lavanya paused for some time and then said, '*Not really.*'

Gayatri decided, '*Then I suggest we should try Faridabad first.*'

'*Are you sure?*'

'My instict says this should be it. Also if none other offers all these facilities, then I would say 101%, we should hit this agency first.'

Lavanya thought for a moment and pulled her mobile to check further the reviews and details about the agencies. She did her analysis and stopped the auto driver.

She said, '*Bhaiya, aap Faridabad ke liye turn kar loge please?*' *(Bhaiya, please take a turn for Faridabad.)*

The driver got irritated and stopped at the roadside.

He grumpily said, '*Kya Madamji, kahan jane ko hai?*' *(What Madam, where do you want to go?)*

They echoed together, '*Faridabad.*'

Auto driver was ready to argue, '*Abhi to Karol Bagh jane ka tha aapko.*' *(But you just said Karol Bagh)*

Again a duet echo, '*Par ab Faridabad jana hai.*' *(But now we want to go to Faridabad.)*

Auto driver took the opportunity and said, '*500 rupaye lagenge.*' *(It will take Rs. 500)*

Gayatri was aghast, '*500 to bahut zyada hain. Thik-thik laga lo. Sector 1 wala market jana hai.*' *(500 is too much. Take what's reasonable. We have to go to Sector 1 Market.)*

Auto driver was adamant too. '*500 se ek paisa kam nahi. Chalna hai to bolo.*' *(I won't take anything less than 500. Now you decide whether you want to go or not.)*

'*Thik hai bhaiya chalo*' *(Okay bhaiya, let's go.)*

Lavanya stopped Gayatri from arguing further.

***

Ishita was lying on the wooden bed and the massage girl, Pinky was with her in that same dimly lit room.

'*How have you been here?*'

'*I am here for the past 2 years. I belong to a village near Ranchi. There was a man from our village who told my father that there was a lot of good work in Delhi and he should send me to Delhi to earn money.*

I have two sisters and one brother, all younger to me. My father is a daily wager for the agriculture farms. We are always in a hand-to-mouth situation. There have even been days when we had to sleep empty stomach. My father sent me with that man and I think he gave some money to my father also.'

Tears were rolling down her eyes as she was speaking with Ishita.

'*Where do you stay these days?*'

'*We come in a van to the hotel and go back to a shelter home.*'

'*Where is the shelter home?*'

'*I don't know exactly but it takes an hour in the van and we are not allowed to open the windows which are all tinted.*'

Pinky continued, '*The shelter home is a huge area. There we have separate cells; a strict caretaker along with his assistants are there to look after us.*'

'*Do they behave badly with you?*'

'*We just have to follow them; if we don't, we can't see them anymore.*'

'*Can't see them anymore? What does that mean?*'

There was a knock on the door and a familiar voice came from outside, '*Pinky, are you done?*'

Pinky quickly wiped her tears, '*Yes, didi.*

'*Ishita ma'am, please do not tell these things to anyone, else I don't know what will happen with me.*'

Ishita got up and lovingly ran her hand over Pinky's head as if she was blessing her with a firm promise in her eyes.

'*Your steam bath is ready.*' Pinky made her sit in the steam bath chamber and left the room. While sitting in the steam bath, she was recalling all that the girl had just told her but was confused whether she was telling her the truth or not.

***

Lavanya and Gayatri stopped outside the agency. It was just a small agency with a table and a chair along with a wooden bench beside. There was no one in there.

Lavanya enquired with the nearby shopkeepers and a man with a heavily built came over.

He asked, '*Kya chahiye madam ji?' (What do you want, madam?)*

'*Are you the owner of the agency?*' Lavanya questioned with attitude.

'*Yes, what happened?*' The owner spoke in a Haryanvi accent.

'*What man, your guys are not working properly at hotel gates?*' Lavanya said angryly.

'*Where ma'am? Please come and sit.*' The owner humbled, welcomed them inside and pulled chairs for them to sit on.

He then asked, '*Now, please tell me what happened?*'

Lavanya started, '*Your guys are not working properly and*

are not punctual at hotel Lalita.'

'No ma'am that should not be the case. Our bouncers are well trained in threatening people and handling unwanted disturbances.'

Lavanya acted surprised, '*Bouncers? Do they really are? They don't behave like them certainly.*'

The man said, '*Yes ma'am. They are there 24/7 in three shifts. I do monitor them.*'

Gayatri added her bit, '*We don't see them at the main gate.*'

'*Main gate? 1 second ma'am,*' the owner pulled out a register to look for details.

He turned over pages and then stopped at one page and turned to them.

'Have a look ma'am. Last time Ranveer sir only placed the bouncers at 4 locations—the spa, the back gate, the laundry, and the basement. That's it. No main gate is mentioned here.'

Gayatri was the first to give away, '*Oh okay.*'

Lavanya handled the situation and said, '*But please convey to your guys to be more vigilant and attentive.*'

'Definitely ma'am, I will take care. Kindly convey to Ranveer Soni sir that last month's payment is due.'

'Sure, thank you.'

'Tea/Coffee, anything for you ma'am?'

'No, it's okay, we will make a move now.'

Gayatri and Lavanya silently got up and stepped out.

'Where is your car, ma'am?'

Lavanya replied cleverly, '*Oh! We actually left the driver; we would take a cab, not an issue.*'

'Shall I drop you to the hotel?'

'*No, it's okay.*' And they rushed off.

They were full-on with their acting skills and did not let the owner know that they were trying to get some information out of him. Soon they came out of the sight of the owner. Gayatri gave a pat on Lavanya's back, '*Lavanya you were too good.*'

They both exchanged smiles.

Lavanya said, '*Come, let's get some coffee.*' They walked to the nearest CCD; Lavanya's favourite hangout.

Gayatri sat and said, '*So dear, there are four areas where we have bouncers in the hotel, and that's exactly why these are the most suspicious areas in the hotel.*'

Lavanya sipped her cappuccino and replied, '*Yes Gayatri. This seems to be quite big. We need to think about it properly.*'

'*Hmm... this doesn't seem to be simple. It is getting complicated now.*'

At the moment her phone rang.

'*Hi Amit, how are you and Ishita?*'

'*Ishita is missing. Can you guys come back to the hotel please?*' Amit said in a fretful voice from the other side.

'*What!? We are coming right now!*'

Gayatri pulled Lavanya and rushed out.

***

CHAPTER 20

DAY TWO CONTINUES...

It was 3:00 p.m. Amit was searching for Ishita. Two of the attendants in the Spa said that she had left the Spa long before.

Amit was calling her but her phone was switched off. He went back to the room but she was not there. He called up the reception from his room and informed them that Ishita is missing from Spa and requested them to inform him in case they happen to find her.

He was sweating profusely and was extremely worried. He could not think of anything but try to recall the sequence of events one by one.

The boys; Rachit, Gaurav and Abhay reached his room, and Amit narrated the story to them.

'*Don't worry, she would be fine, and we will find her.*' Rachit consoled Amit.

'*The point is we can't tell anyone that we were spying the place or it might cause more danger to her.*' Amit was almost in tears.

Rachit offered to help, '*Let's go and check the place again.*'

'*Do you think we should call the police?*' Abhay suggested.

There was a moment of silence.

'I think so,' Amit said with some courage, *'I can't let her be in trouble. I don't know where she is and how she is...'*

Gaurav agreed with Amit, *'Also we now know there definitely is something fishy here and it's not small. It could be much bigger than our imagination.'*

Amit told them, *'Lavanya and Gayatri are on their way. Richa is in the room. I haven't told her yet.'*

Rachit proposed, *'Let's wait for them to reach here and from now onwards let us be together and well connected.'*

Abhay added, *'With this case, it might happen that the culprits now know that we are aware of the mischief happening here.'*

By the next hour, Lavanya, Gayatri, and Richa had joined the boys in Ishita's room. It was almost evening now. It had been more than 3 hours now that Ishita was missing. They all gathered together to step up for their next move. A swift plan of action drifted.

Amit explained, *'Two of us will reach the spa and if possible, check for the CCTV clippings*. Others can take help from the reception and try to look for her in other areas of the hotel.'

Gaurav said, *'Abhay's uncle is in the police. Let's call him and take his help. Abhay, let's launch a missing complaint about her with the area police.'*

Amit and Rachit went to the Spa again and enquired.

They could see her entry in the register. They spoke to few of the massage girls but could not get any clue. Rachit's eyes reached for the CCTV and enquired about the clippings. But to their surprise, the response they got was – *'It was not working.'*

In the meanwhile, the bouncers at the Spa gate peeped in and requested politely, *'Sir, Ma'am might have gone somewhere else, please have a look into the hotel. She was not here. Our other customers are waiting, kindly excuse. We will inform you if we get any information.'*

Both of them did not say anything but left the place.

They both were silent. They could sense that this could be much bigger and dangerous than they had ever thought of. They could figure out that the bouncers could be more dangerous to them and they should find a different approach to handle this otherwise even they might get caught in this risk and then there would be no way they would have saved Ishita.

***

It was a small room, painted white from inside. There was a small painting of Radha and Krishna nailed on the left sidewall. A wooden cupboard beside with keys hanging out of it was placed adjacent to the painting. On the right side, there was a square window with white plain curtains drawn. It was breezy outside for some of the cool breeze was coming inside making the curtains flow.

She was lying on the bed amidst this surrounding in a white cotton gown, covered with a soft white blanket. She could see the front door was closed and beside the door, there was a small reading table and a lady sitting there and reading something. She could see only her back. The lady was also in a white suit with a dupatta covering her head.

Further, beside the table at another corner of the room, there was a door, it must be the washroom.

She could hardly utter a word but could find a covered glass near her bedside. She managed to lift herself to get the glass but the steel cover fell with a clang.

The lady turned back.

'Didi, you woke up! You need water? Wait, I will get it for you.'

Ishita tried to recognize that lady but it was actually a girl who must have been around 15-16 years old. The girl poured some water in the glass from an earthen pot placed beside it.

Handing over the glass to her, she said, '*Didi, how are you feeling now? How did you come here?*'

Ishita took a few sips of water and was able to regain her voice, '*Where am I? How did I come here? And I think I have seen you, who are you?*'

'*Yes didi! Don't you recognize me; you got me water in your hotel room.*'

Ishita quickly recalled that incident. She was glad it had actually happened and she had not just imagined it. '*Damn! You are the girl who jumped from the window. Thank God you are safe. But when we reached downstairs you were not there.*'

Thinking about that event, tears rolled down from the girl's eyes. She still had that wound on her head and her head was wrapped in a bandage. Also, there were brushes on her arms and face.

She hugged the girl. '*What is your name? I am Ishita.*'

'*My name is Seema.*'

'*Seema, what is this place? How did I reach here? I was actually in the Spa steam chamber and I don't remember how I came here and where are my clothes and...*'

'*Hold on! I think I got it now; they might have brought you here; exactly how I came here.*'

Ishita was shocked.

Seema started with her story -

'*I belong to Amravati and was traveling on a train to Nagpur for my entrance exam. I was sitting in the train and reading something, not sure if I ate or drank something, and much later when I opened my eyes I was here– it felt like I was in deep sleep for years. I have not met my parents since then and I could not get out of this place since then. It's been a year now. That day, I got a chance to escape and somehow managed to reach your room but the room boy saw me, I did not want to go back so I thought of ending my life and I jumped out of the window but look at my fate, I am still alive.*'

Ishita hugged her and caressed her on her head to console her but she had sheer anger in her eyes.

'Didi, how did you land here?' All of a sudden Seema interrupted.

Ishita thought hard, *'As far as I remember, I was in the spa, I was with Pinky and she was massaging me. She also had a similar story to tell but she couldn't share much.'*

Seema was trying to connect the dots.

Ishita continued, *'Then I think somebody called her to wind up and she quickly put me in the steam chamber and left. After that, I am here. I don't know how I came here and who changed my clothes. I am a bit worried; hope nothing wrong happened with me.'*

'No Didi, till now you are safe but I am not sure for how long. I was in the same cab that was used to transfer an unconscious you to this ashram.'

'Oh! Is this the same place about which Pinky was talking about?'

Seema seemed confused. *'Maybe, not sure. But Di, this is just not an ashram but a Devil's Workshop.'*

Ishita had anger, anxiety, angst, a clamor for justice everything in her eyes all at once. But not fear. She had elevated above it. Fear usually was related to physical damage, pain or fear of death. She had experienced them all and now she had no fear left in her.

But at the same time, her second thought was giving her some indication if the girl was telling the truth. Coming from a safety trainer background, she was able to figure out the danger as well as the correctness of the whole scenario.

Still, she was curious to know her story as she had to somehow escape from that place. By now she understood that the steam had some medicine that made her unconscious. So now she was cautious about any smoke or smell.

Seema continued her story, *'Shahab ji's assistant was*

trying to drag you into his room but somehow I convinced him that since you are not in a good shape, I should make you ready and he agreed and thus you landed here.'

Ishita could clearly make out things were quite big, and she could foresee that she had to somehow find out a way to escape from here and help all these women too, but for that she had to make the first move.

Ishita took a deep breath, '*Seema would you help me for youself, myself and all other such girls who are caged here forcefully, away from their homes and family?*'

Seema had tears in her. She could just manage an affirmative nod.

Ishita wiped her eyes with her warm hands. '*Get up and bring a pen and paper if you have any.*'

Seema pulled up the mattress and took out a small diary and a pencil.

'*This is what I have stolen from the hotel; we are not allowed to keep any.*'

'*Well done.*' Ishita encouraged her. '*Now can you help me to draw the map of this ashram?*'

Seema started scribbling some structures and showed her some important points like Sahabji who seemed to be the owner of this ashram who had got links with some big politicians and industrialists. There were around 60–70 such cottages in this ashram with somewhere around 250- 300 occupancy.

'*This is quite huge.*' Ishita was worried.

Seema continued, '*If you follow the left corner of this cottage and keep moving, you can see a big cottage to your right, that's Sahabji's residence and the meditation center. From behind that place you can see a road with trees on both sides. That would lead you to the main gate.*

This is all I know. Beyond the gate, I haven't been ever.'

After having some water, Seema continued, '*We get*

picked up and dropped back after attendance from the meditation center. For us, shopping means the two shops near the canteen, one for clothes and accessories, the other for things required by women- like pads and undergarments and important medicines. And everyone can't get things from there. Ramesh, an assistant of Shahab ji decides for us. Since I received some big tip from one of my clients, I was given this single occupancy for 3 months.'

Ishita understood many of the things.

There was a knock at the door.

Seema whispered, might be someone to take you.

Ishita quickly dressed up by borrowing a salwar kurta from Seema and took a position behind the door and tore the curtain to form a cloth ball at the corner. She then stood ready for attack.

Seema opened the door, as soon as the man entered, Ishita kicked his leg from behind and made the man fall on the floor. Seema closed the door behind him. Ishita jumped on the fallen man over his back and pulled his head up by grabbing his hair and covered his nose with the ball of cloth.

Within seconds, the man was unconscious. Then they both dragged him and pushed him under the bed.

'*Wow di, what was that?*' Seema was amazed.

'*Chloroform, my girl.*' Ishita smiled.

Seema was excited and hugged Ishita in an emotional impulse.

'*You are a genius, di.*'

'*Don't waste time, just grab your important belongings and let's move towards the gate now.*'

Seema pulled the bed sheet off, put her diary, some books, and a few photographs in the middle and wrapped it to form a shoulder bag with knots.

Then Ishita pulled the curtain rod down and asked Seema to hold it. They put off the lights and left the room. They followed the path crossing other girls' rooms; their similar dresses helped them to escape easily. They reached the meditation center when one of the ladies appeared out of nowhere and stopped them.

'*Hey girl, what is this you are carrying?*' The lady inquired pointing to the bed sheet bag supported by the rod.

'*Nothing ma'am, I am on my period and my sheets, and clothes got dirty, I need to drop them to the laundry.*'

'*Hmm...*' the lady left.

'*What's that?*' Ishita enquired

'*Here we have to declare when we have menstrual dates. We have to get our names entered in the register and show the dirty clothes to get sanitary pads; otherwise they don't give us anything. It is disgusting when the male guards write our names in the register.*'

Seema was feeling really bad to know about the pathetic situation the girls were living in.

Ishita said, '*It's really horrible but don't worry dear we will get them exposed.*'

'*It's not that easy.*'

'*I know, but let's have faith.*'

They moved ahead. Ishita was quite vigilant throughout the way. She could figure out a CCTV camera placed on one of the trees. Ishita knew how to make herself safe from CCTV. She directed Seema into the blind spot and they moved accordingly.

Soon they were near the main gate. Now they had to jump out of this gate on the main road. But there were four guards guarding that gate.

Seema was a bit worried, '*Didi, how are we going to get rid of these four guards.*'

'*I have a plan!*' Ishita murmured into Seema's ears.

Then they both started with a mock fight of pushing each other and addressing each other with abusive words. They dramatized the fight enough to catch the guards' attention. Two of the guards walked towards them to know about the scandal. Ishita mockingly came closer to both the guards and tried to lure them with seductive facial expressions and gestures. She gesticulated the guards to come behind the tree trunk.

The guards waved the consent of handling the issue to the other two guards and followed the two ladies behind the tree.

Seema made one of the guards to come close to her face and lips and she suddenly pushed the chloroformed cloth in front of the guard's nose. She was also prepared to hold her breath until the guard became unconscious.

Meanwhile, behind another tree, Seema did the same with the other guard.

So two of the four guards were down and unconscious

Ishita now pulled her ear studs and gave one to Seema.

They then started calling the other two guards and urged them to come and check the two guards. The other two came rushing and left the gates unattended. As soon as the guards came closer, both the girls with all their might kicked the guards in their groin, and when the two guards fell to the ground, they again put some chloroform onto their mouths and got them unconscious within seconds.

Seema soon checked the pocket of the guard to pull out his handkerchief and stuffed it in his mouth so that he could not speak. They took off their shirts and tied their hands behind them with the dupattas.

Behind the tree, both the girls quickly wore the guard uniforms over what they were wearing and walked towards the gate. Since the gate was open and the CCTV could capture the guards' uniform only, Ishita and Seema reached the gate, pushed it open and started walking outside. After a few meters they began running for their dear lives.

Seema: *'Didi, how come you have chloroform with you?'*

Ishita- *'The day I realized something was wrong in the hotel and I myself got unconscious when I thought you had died, I got one from the nearby market; thinking that just in case I am not able to fight someone, I can always use this. I couldn't put it in my purse otherwise my husband would know, so I put it in the small moisturizer bottle from the hotel and tie it in a pouch around my bangles. Nobody noticed it.'*

***

CHAPTER 21

THE SEARCH

It was around 3:00 a.m; the demon's hour. Abhay and Gaurav were sitting at the police station. Abhay's legs had started tingling due to being in one position for long. Mild irritation and deep furrows were getting gathered on his eyebrows. Abhay moved his legs to give them a break and raised his voice a little to say, '*Can any of you please lodge our complaint. A lady is missing, and this is a really serious matter.*'

His voice got the attention of everyone sitting over there.

One of the men in uniform looked up to Abhay with his widened eyes; he had his name written in pure Hindi on a rectangular batch clipped over to the left side of his chest. He pushed his chair back with a creaking noise, rose up from his wooden seat and staggered himself towards Abhay and Gaurav.

'*Janab listen, we can't lodge a complaint unless it is 24 hours of missing. Do you understand?*' Suddenly, the muttering voice had become loud and clear.

He tapped on Abhay's shoulder and said, '*Control young man! She might have gone somewhere or might have had a fight with her husband.*' The cop consoled him and went outside to have his betel quid.

Gaurav consoled Abhay and insinuated him to make a move now.

They both went out. Since it was quite dark outside,

they could hardly find any conveyance. They started walking. There was a deep silence between them. Suddenly, the phone rang. It was Abhay's uncle calling.

'*Hello, Uncle. I hope I did not disturb you this late in the night.*'

'*No, not at all son; what happened? You were calling me at this odd hour. Is everything fine?*'

'*Actually uncle...*'

Abhay tried to narrate the long story short.

'*Which hotel did you mention?*'

'*Hotel Lalita Palace.*'

'*Where are you guys now?*'

'*We are outside of the police station near Connaught Place.*

'*Ok, let me speak with the officer in-charge over there to drop you to my place.*'

Within 10 minutes, one of the constables approached them in his jeep, '*Sirs, Singhal Sir has told me to drop you to his place. Please get in the car.*'

In about 20 minutes, they reached Abhay's Singhal Uncle's residence.

The early morning chirping of the birds was quite prominent. The air had a stint of flowery aroma. It had been almost dawn now- the sky was dark blue and the sun was cracking orange.

They pulled the gate and walked through the cemented pavement inside a well-maintained house in Civil Lines. On the right side was a walled boundary and the left was a green, grassy, flowery and leafy fenced lawn. Mr Singhal was sitting in his open porch where his office was set up with cane chairs and table and was having his cup of black coffee. Two of the policemen were accompanying him with some conversation.

Uncle paused as he took a glance at the boys and alluded to the other policemen to leave.

'Come, boys, have a seat. Need some coffee?'

He was sitting with a wireless bell and rang it to call his help for two coffees.

'Uncle ji, could you please help us find Ishita? We hope that she is fine.' Abhay requested.

'How come you guys got into all this?' Uncle was surprised to know that they were here and asking for help to fight a gang.

Abhay narrated the whole story elaborately from beginning till now. Uncle called up someone and within no time a handsome, tall man was there to meet them.

'Good morning Sir,' he gave a perfect triumphant salute.

'Meet Abhay and Gaurav.' He introduced the two friends and waved his hand towards a chair to indicate him to sit with them.

'And boys, he is Abhimanyu Sampath, Inspector, Crime Branch. He also looks after the crime against women cell.'

Inspector Abhimanyu shook hands with them as he joined them over the table. They had a brief conversation which included Gaurav to show their group chats and photographs that they had shared over the common WhatsApp group. Inspector Abhimanyu quickly called up a few other police cops to initiate a search for Ishita.

Gaurav and Abhay took their uncle's leave to accompany Inspector Abhimanyu and be a part of the search team.

Back in the hotel, Lavanya and Gayatri started with the clandestine forage of any clue behind Ishita's vanishing. Amit was in total distress for not being able to find his beloved wife, he desperately searched the various locations of the hotel.

They all communicated periodically and checked for updates over WhatsApp chats.

And back in the woods, Ishita and Seema were still running. They were thirsty, exhausted and completely clueless as to where they were heading. It was a dark, dry and dusty mud track long enough for only a single four-wheeler to pass. The track was fenced with dry bushes whose branches sometimes scratched the girls.

They got bruised and wounded on their arms and legs as they were traversing along.

'*Di, I can't run anymore.*' Seema panted.

'*Beta, a little more, the main road seems to be near.*' Ishita held her hand and pulled forward. The two women had been running for a long time. They did not even have time to take a breath. They just wanted to get away from that hell.

They could see the road now within a few leaps.

Soon, both the lassies landed on a proper road. They halted to take a big sigh.

'*Which way should we select to proceed?*' The turn of the face towards the right was an omen for Ishita.

A tempo truck came with speed and hit Ishita and it was gone in no time.

'*Diiii!!*' a loud scream echoed from Seema.

Everything froze. It was a terrible moment.

Ishita was lying on the road in a pool of blood. The noticeable red blood was flowing over the concrete road from her left, her eyes were closed and her beautiful fair face was covered with blood. Seema tried to tap on her shoulder, '*Dii, Wake up!! Wake up!!*'

The other moment, she was screaming aloud, '*Somebody help please...*'

She ran on the road from one side to another to stop a vehicle, '*Please stop!! Please help!!*'

'*Somebody... help!!*'

'*Somebody... help!!*'

***

CHAPTER 22

DAY THREE

'*Ishita!!*' Gayatri screamed, all of a sudden.

'*What happened, Gayatri?*' Lavanya tried to get a hold of her as they were trying to spy on the 5th-floor corridor of the hotel.

'*We have to reach for her soon, she needs us. Ishita needs us.*' Gayatri became desperate.

'*Gayatri, what are you saying? We are trying to find her only.*' Lavanya became curious.

'*Please call Amit and Gaurav, we need to take help from the police. She is not here.*' Gayatri alarmed.

She was trembling and somewhere deep inside she had gotten a clue that something was terribly wrong with Ishita and if they did not hurry, things would worsen.

They all decided to meet at a common point in the city.

It was almost afternoon by then.

It was an old broken garage, somewhere near Mehrauli, a place in the southwest region of Delhi. The place withstands one of the huge brick-slender towers, a well-known heritage of Delhi–the Qutub Minar.

They all stood in a circle facing each other.

'*Sir, Ishita is in trouble now. I can sense she has met with some accident and she is in some hospital.*'

'*How do you know? Did she call you or text you?*' Inspector

Abhimanyu enquired.

'*Could you sense any clue related to where we should head up?*' Lavanya understood her.

Inspector Abhimanyu was confused but said, '*Hospitals are an option to search, but there are no clues in the CCTV of the exit doors of the hotel. She must be inside the hotel somewhere. I think we should have a deeper search there.*'

'*No Sir, there are hidden entry and exit doors in this hotel. We have found something mysterious in the hotel Spa. Ishita must have found something, that's why she is in trouble now. Please help Sir, My wife is missing. I know she is bold, she is a black belt, but still...*' Amit sobbed.

Gaurav held Amit to console him.

'*Sir, do you have any idea of a hospital that has a mother Mary statue in a glass chamber on the top floor of the building?*' Gayatri suddenly blurted.

'Okay… *let me think- There are St. Mary, Holy Faith, Jolly Good, Get Well Soon hospitals which are handled by Christians.*' Abhimanyu said.

Lavanya already started googling to come up with more options.

She showed the pictures of the hospitals on their website to Gayatri for verification.

'*It seems to be Jolly Good hospital!' Gayatri suddenly pointed out.*

Abhimanyu was surprised to find the exactly similar structure as mentioned by Gayatri, which astonished him, but he kept quiet.

'*So for now, I suppose we should head fast to the hospital and find Ishita.*' Lavanya stood up.

Lavanya used her technology skills to find out the area, the time it might take to reach there. She found the hospital numbers and enquired for Ishita, since the name was not familiar with the hospital, they could not suggest accurately, but she got to know that there were a few accidental cases early in the morning and one of them is a lady.

Two Innovas were heading towards the hospital now. Everyone was equally worried for Ishita. They all prayed for her life and safety. Meanwhile Gaurav and Rachit were consoling Amit, who was still in tears.

'*Sir, I just checked the nearby areas on Google for that hospital.*' Lavanya was still trying to find clues for the puzzling conundrums.

'*See Rachit, there has been a big area marked in maps which says Sahabji Anath Ashram.*' Lavanya showed Rachit.

'*Yeah, there is an ashram, I suppose, but I think it is not a very known one.*' Inspector Abhimanyu responded.

'*Please check the boundary marked by Google, it seems to be a quite huge area inside.*' Lavanya claimed.

Looking at Google maps, Abhimanyu scratched his beard and ordered, '*Rane, can you find out about this Ashram? It seems to have somewhere around 20 acres of boundary.*'

'*I need to have all unknown and unearthed facts, basically the–kachcha chitta–of the guru and this ashram.*'

Now everyone was searching and Googling about the ashram and Sahabji guru.

Some found his pictures, some found his preaching recordings and some found his links with political and business tycoons over the internet. Nowadays, the internet has been a saviour most of the times. In about an hour's travel, they reached the hospital. Lavanya, Gayatri, Amit leaped out to run fast to meet Ishita.

They reached the reception and asked the receptionist if there is a girl named Ishita admitted.

The receptionist guided them based on the description and queries. The three of them rushed as directed and came to the room where Ishita was lying down. The floor reception suggested the visitor time was from 5.00 p.m so they should come back during that time. But with multiple requests, the nurse allowed one person.

Amit was the first one to visit her in the emergency ward.

She had got bandages over her head and some over her arms.

There was a plaster in her left arm. Thankfully, the truck did not drive over her legs.

She seemed to be fast asleep.

Amit anxiously enquired about her health with the ward nurse and was relieved with the response that she was fine and was out of any danger. It was just that she was given some pain killers and antibiotics to reduce the pain that had a sedative effect on her.

The police tried to enquire about the accident with the doctors. Then they decided to go and uncover the facts at the accident spot and file a case accordingly.

Amit, Lavanya, and Gayatri stayed back in the hospital to take care of Ishita.

The boys followed the police to the spot. They spoke to the shopkeepers of the vicinity but couldn't find any eyewitness for the accident.

Also, no CCTV could be figured.

***

CHAPTER 23

DAY FOUR

Some streaks of glittery sunlight were peeping through the windows and alluring the bright face of Ishita.

Signs of remembrance were visible in her eyes. With some struggle and stress, she was able to open her eyes. Amit was sitting beside her and was echoing her name with love.

Amit gave a big smile and showed his consent with his eyes that '*Everything's fine.*'

She smiled and pulled his palm towards her face to blow it a kiss.

'*Take rest Ishi. I am here now.*' Amit showed his promising existence by following a kiss on her forehead and gently keeping his palm over her head. The doctor came in for his morning visit and gave a green signal for her discharge in the next few hours. It was just that she had to keep her arm plastered for the next one month.

'It's a miracle that even though she got hit by a truck, she isn't critically injured. She was smart enough to roll her legs towards her stomach, hide her face with her hands and somehow push her body away from the moving truck.' Said the doctor.

Ishita narrated her story to Amit and her friends and mentioned about Seema, the girl she had met the other day in the hotel room and how she had saved her from that ashram.

'*Ashram... that Sahabji's one, which is visible in the Google maps? OMG!*' Lavanya was confounded.

'*Maybe we should tell all this to Abhimanyu Sir.*' Gaurav claimed.

'*By the way, where is she? Did you guys meet her?*' Ishita wanted to know about Seema.

'*No, she was not here when we came and even the hospital people just mentioned that a group of people brought you here.*' Gayatri informed.

Ishita could not digest this, '*But we were together when we fled from the ashram. That's really strange. Where could Seema go?*'

'*What's strange?*' Inspector Abhimanyu was there to get Ishita's statement.

'*How are you, the bold and beautiful?*' Inspector Abhimanyu initiated his conversation.

'*I am fine, sir. Thank you.*'

He was introduced to Ishita who told him in detail about what had happened last night when she was in trouble.

'*Thank you, sir.*' Amit expressed his deep gratitude to Inspector Abhimanyu after.

'*Can you get her sketch for us? That girl Seema's?*'

'*Yes of course. I remember her completely.*' Ishita's voice was quite promising.

Inspector Abhimanyu instructed one of his cops to find a sketch artist and get the sketch done. Also, he instructed to circulate it into all Delhi NCR police stations and outstations too for some shred of evidence. Also, he instructed to offer them a stay at some guest house with some protections and requested them not to move alone or visit the hotel alone.

* * *

It was a quiet afternoon but the Girl Gang was calculating their days' plan. They knew their day 4 was getting through.

Everybody was silent. Yet the background processor was running all the system jobs simultaneously.

Inspector Abhimanyu dropped around to visit them.

He was there with some devious stratagem. He got all of them to sit around a round table so that he could deliver the role-play.

'*Guys, first of all, thank you for being a good citizen of the country and trying to help the country to kick off the dirt and dust; helping us maintain its sanity. We need more aware and passionate people like you, who are not just interested in their welfare but also the welfare of other citizens.*' He showed his gratitude to these young minds and the shield-maidens.

'*And now I need you guys to form a team and perform a sting operation.*'

Everyone was silent with their eyes and ears on alert.

'*Operation Red-Escape.*'

***

The hotel Lalita Palace was standing exotic in its ambiance and attire. It was around 8 p.m. The boys' group entered the hotel to get to the restaurant.

They grouped up, chortle and giggled up noisily while entering into the restaurant. They behaved in a very loud and flippant manner, getting all the attention they could. They moved to the bar counter and checked out for drinks. Their carefree attitude was slowly getting noticed.

The boys were Amit, Rachit, Gaurav, and Abhay. They were in a loud facial disguise so that nobody could recognize them.

Amit went to the bartender and whispered slowly, '*Where to find some nice gigolettes?*'

The bartender looked at him and then got back to his work without any reaction.

Gaurav went up to Amit, taking a small peg of a Jim

Beam whiskey; he smiled and waved his palm in a top to down motion and acclaimed, *'fulljhariyan... kake!' (Sexy women, brother!)*

The bartender again looked at him and this time he finally left the counter.

Amit and Gaurav gave a loud laugh and got back to the table where Rachit and Abhay were already sitting and having their drinks. This time it was the boys' gang who was on a mission.

On one hand, they were nervous and the other brawny side of theirs was giving them a sense of empiricism and positivism.

A lean thin man walked to their table. He pulled a chair and leaned forward towards the table to throw his words in a mere low voice.

'4 ghante–5 sikke–chalega?' (4 hours- 5 coins, would that do?)

They were all quiet for a moment as if the words were a bouncer to them. The man was actually giving them some clues for which they were here. But looking at the boys' facial expression, the man reframed his words.

'*Oh okay, it is 4 hours and 5000 bucks, fine?*' He explained.

'*Okay*', Amit replied.

'*Money right now.*'

Amit pulled the cash out of his wallet and placed it on the table. The guy took the money, hid the notes in his shirt cuffs and stood up.

'*Where?*' Amit enquired.

'*I will be back in an hour,*' the man claimed and left.

Amit took his mobile to type a text -

The fish got hooked onto the bait. It's time to hit the iron.

He sent it to Inspector Abhimanyu.

As per the plan, they checked the camera buttons on

their mobile and the guy's picture got captured. Rachit had sent the same to Inspector Abhimanyu. Now they were ready for the shootings. They snooped about their button cameras secretly to get some quick snaps.

The man was back within 40 minutes.

He had 4 keys with him. They were room keys. He handed over one to each of them.

'*6th floor in the next 15 minutes.*' He mentioned and left.

They knew that they had to capture as much information they could without any clue as to who they were dealing with and of course without a single touch to the ladies. Without knowing much about the other party, the boys were on a go.

They went about their mission–Red-Escape.

A mixed feeling of pride that they were a part of some mission and the woeful feeling for the plight of the women floated in their minds. Each one of them unlocked their respective rooms and the girls were already there. They walked in slowly and were clear in mind that they needed to manage without any suspicion at least for an hour or so.

'*Mission abort. Walkout. Meet you at Sir's residence.*' A message beeped on their phones

They got perplexed. They left their rooms and looked at each other.

Some guards tried to stop them. They were the bouncers, '*You can't go like this.*'

The other one said, 'S*earch them.*'

Rachit gave a hard punch to one of the bouncers to leap forward.

And then in no time, the boys were trying to fight the bouncers standing outside. They knew there was no other way to escape from here. Amit sat on a bouncer who tried to punch Rachit back, while Gaurav and Abhay fought the other bouncer- both of them were trying to jump on him and pin him down.

While all this mess was going on a group of policemen in civil dress came there to conduct a raid of the hotel. All the doors were knocked open and around 15 men and girls were rescued. Some of them were really in an abysmal and dreadful condition. The girls were as young as 12 years of age and were shivering with fear, some of the girls had bruises on their faces and hands- many started crying the moment they saw the policemen, not realizing what would happen next.

The police had covered all the major open and hidden exit points of the hotel and the floor on which the boys were fighting were also covered. The police came to fight with these bouncers. Meanwhile women constables were rescuing the girls and carefully taking them away through the lift, trying to make them feel comfortable and safe.

One of the policemen came up to the boys and shook hands with them.

'*Thank you. Abhimanyu Sir told me to drop you to Singhal Sir's residence. Please come.*'

There was a sense of satisfaction on each of their faces which was easily visible.

Amit opened his mobile to make a call to Inspector Abhimanyu.

Then he read his message again and confused said, '*Why did Sir mention that the mission is aborted when they have already caught the Johns and the girls?*'

'*Yeah, you are right. It should be something like mission completed or accomplished.*' Rachit said surprised.

***

CHAPTER 24

DAY FIVE, THE CONCLUSION

This time the clock was showing the hour's needle at 2 and the minute's on 3. The second's needle was crazily rotating as if an animal had been tethered in the oiler.

The room was a big conference hall. A big oval-shaped wooden table surrounded with 26 chairs. The head chair was occupied by Singhal Sir and on the left side 8 chairs were occupied by other policemen, some were in uniform and some in civil dress. On the right side, the chairs were occupied by the Girls Gang.

Everybody sat silently

The lights were dim, but everyone's faces could be recognized.

The boys entered the room along with the Inspector who had raided the hotel. The inspector entered and straightaway reached Singhal Sir seated at the seat opposite to the entrance door and stood in attention to give him a salute.

'Sir, all of them have been caught and held at Mehrauli police station as of now.'

'That's good.' Singhal Sir signalled towards a chair and directed him to have a seat.

'Boys have your seat; you all have done a great job. Well done!'

The broadened-with-pride-chested boys dragged their respective chairs to settle down and join the round table.

And then Shalini entered the room.

'*Welcome Inspector Shalini! Well done! Come and have your seat.*'

Everyone moved their heads towards the entrance door. Everyone was surprised to see the receptionist from the hotel who was the first person to recognize the girls on the magazine cover page. She stood there in full police uniform.

'*So thank you all for being a part of this mission. I want you all to know about this mission of which each one of you was an integral part.*' Singhal Sir stood up from his chair and took a long breath and started the background of the story.

'*We had some clue from one of our informers about some illegal happenings in the hotel. So inspector Abhimanyu and inspector Shalini took the charge to handle the case properly. Shalini joined as receptionist and Abhimanyu was helping her from outside. She happened to find the cover girls coincidentally reaching the hotel at the same time. Although I don't believe in coincidence but later on whatever happened with the cover girls and the boys was a fortunate stroke of serendipity. All happened by chance but was good for all of us.*

Shalini took the opportunity to make you guys present around circumstances where you could smell something fishy. And you guys are brave enough to plunge into all this, even putting your life at risk. I would rather call these girls as warriors, shield-warriors.

I wish every citizen could behave similarly.'

The suspense was growing in everyone to know more about this case. One after one, the scenes where Shalini was directing the girls to look over the areas like laundry, spa were sliding in front of their eyes. All of them thought and figured that Shalini was actually present in every important development of their findings.

Singhal Sir then continued further -

'When you guys came to me, I was already aware of many things happening in the hotel except the fact that Ishita got missing but I had let you guys only to find her out and you all did it very well.

Remember, the major clue was Seema's sketch which was suggested by Ishita…

Abhimanyu, do you want to continue next?'

Singhal Sir had now rolled over the ball to Abhimanyu's court and the scoreboard started rolling further up.

'First of all thank you, my friends, for helping me out in cracking this case, I would especially like to thank Gayatri to figure out the hospital where we found Ishita since we were clueless at that time. It had been at a breakneck speed. Then thanks to Lavanya for finding out about the bouncers and the ashram. That actually helped us to validate many things.

So coming back, based on Seema's sketch we were able to find that she had originally been a jailbird. She had been a convict and had been under lifetime imprisonment due to murder charge of her husband or say boyfriend with whom she eloped. For now she too is missing and our team is on a search.'

Everyone was thunderstuck by this piece of news. Especially Ishita, she couldn't believe that someone like Seema who was herself caught in a deadly scam could do something like this in her past.

'Then Lavanya mentioned about the security guard's details, we went there and found a few more sketches and photographs of girls and further digging helped us find out about more of the imprisoned girls and women. Also, about few more who were related to men and women who were under imprisonment; I mean their kins and comrades and especially kids.

Then, based on Singhal Sir's permission, I got you boys to observe the sting operation and we figured out the prison from where these dealings were working out. Jailor Om Prakash had been detained and few of his supporters were directly caught in the act of letting these men and women escape or be taken for this job. It was a matter of real shame for me for being a people's man and still have somebody like him in our community.

If we as followers of the Indian Constitution are into such crimes, how are we going to curb off prostitution, flesh market or human trafficking from our society?

He then aimed at a middle-aged man sitting in between two of the policemen in uniform.'

Gayatri's ears arose by hearing the word trafficking as that had been her initial sixth sense alarm. Inspector Shalini could not sit back. She got from her seat and directly reached the jailor and gave a loud slap, followed by another and third one in continuation on his face.

There was pin-drop silence in the room.

'*Sorry, Sir!*' She addressed and then went back to her seat.

'*Shalini, the case has been prepared against him and tomorrow morning, I mean today the proceedings will get started. So before the morning news flash, Sir wanted to crack the case in front of his team.*'

Inspector Abhimanyu got interrupted by a raised hand.

'*Yes Ishita, your question please.*'

'*Sir it is really shocking to know about prison prostitution and human trafficking. But I just wanted to know if you have been to that ashram where I have been.*'

'*Yeah, good point. Actually, Seema was a notorious criminal. She tried to escape from the hotel when you saw her falling from the window. She got hurt that day and the jailor could not take her to hospital. So she was taken to the ashram. Since that ashram was quite helpful for women, the jailor made stories and one of his jail assistants had been put her up there and he used to visit her daily to give her medicines. The guy with whom you fought within the ashram was actually a police constable.*'

'*OMG!*' a reaction rolled over from Ishita's mouth.

Amit gave a proud look to his beloved wife.

'*And how did Ishita reach there?*' Another question came

up from Gayatri.

Abhimanyu directed towards Shalini.

'It happened this way, since you and Amit had been out in the hotel questioning, there were two girls in the SPA who moved you out of the hotel, from there the jailor got you into that ashram only because his constable was going to take you out from there and might have warned you or might berate you later on. But they were unaware that a woman like you could be a black belt holder.

For all such activities, there had been two places of escape in the hotel, which you guys have profoundly figured out. One has been through the laundry, through the backyard fire drill stairs from where sometimes the movement of the dry cleaners happen.

The other one is a back door from the spa which draws to the back gate which was mostly closed and covered with a green fence.'

Abhimanyu continued, '*So the ashram had been a really good one, but been be fooled by the jailor. Being a policeman, he used his powers to direct Sahabji. I was really pleased to see ashrams like these which are actually doing good work but get into suspicion due to some other defamed ones. Sahabji thanked us for catching the jailor- he said he tried so many times reaching the police but was always shunned away and threatened. And about that spa girl who got Ishita fainted and also told all lies to Ishita about her life to gain her sympathy. She was also a criminal into long term imprisonment due to multiple theft cases.*

Now about the complicated working process- The Jailor has got Johns and Pimps, they get in touch with the jailor and bring in the clients. The Jailor gets the female prisoners ready for delivery. You won't believe, there is a small tunnel in the prison, which the Jailor opens for any delivery. In custody, we will get to find from him, if there are more officers or other personnel involvements or more such tunnels in the jail. Well, I am pretty sure; there must be some big hands behind which encouraged the Jailor to take such steps. He does not hold enough power to do it on his own.'

'As per our information, the jailor had also been sending

the girls to the dangerous group that runs human trafficking in India- it is called Alfa B- Zone and they are expanding in many other countries too. The other security people you saw in the hotel were the people of this group. Their main head works from Russia. We have caught many of its people in India and will be making them go through extensive enquiry. We cannot give any further information, since this matter is of grave concern to the police and a lot is yet to be discovered. The FBI will be taking over soon. But before any of that happens, I wanted to give you guys a clue of what you all were dealing with.'

'Yes, we need to question the owner of Lalita Palace. He has been to London, I have sent information to him to come back and meet me because it is important that we find out how could such a well-respected hotel be involved in such a serious crime. We don't know yet whether the owner was involved or was completely unaware of this.' added upon Singhal Sir.

So 'cover page shield warriors', I would call you with this name only. Thank you very much once again. Your help has paced up this case to get resolved quicker. We have been working on this case since long and we got many a cues in all these months but none could actually help us catch some prime suspects- we now have the jailor who is locally involved and the security people you saw. We will also be questioning the girls who were captured and seeking whatever help we can from them.'

He came over to three of the girls and shook hands with them. Then to the boys and the meeting dispersed where everyone congratulated and hugged each other.

Abhimanyu directed his policemen to take the jailor to police custody and get the papers ready for him and the press release.

This has been a big case.

They were walking out of the room. Outside of the room, there were around 20 of the girls sitting along squatted on the floor. At other end, some men were caught in the raid and two of the policemen were questioning each of them and jotting down their statements.

Lavanya saw one of the girls got up and spat on the Jailor as he was dragged through handcuffed along the way. She was able to feel the pain the girls might have gone through and how forcefully they were made to do things. One could never imagine the kind of illegal scams happening in the country. Women are not safe anywhere, forget about a place like prison.

Lavanya missed Arshi, she hadn't got a chance to talk to her properly in the last few days. Her little sunshine, her happiness, but she was glad she had Rachit with her now.

Then as the three of them held hand in hand and walked upon, two of the girls came over and held their feet.

'Aap Devi ho, aapne hume bacha liya!' (You are goddess, you saved us.)

Ishita and Gayatri pulled them up and hugged them. All three of them hugged them.

While walking through, Lavanya could identify a little girl sitting over. She walked over to her.

'How old are you?'

'12 years old,' she said.

'She has killed her rapist. The case is going on against her.' One of the constables mentioned.

'That's pathetic, can I take over her case, she might need some help.'

While speaking, she looked at Rachit who was standing at a little distance but could have listened to her words.

Rachit gave a contended nod with a smile.

'I would like to speak with her attendants or parents for her.' Her words got confidence.

***

CHAPTER 25

THE NEWS BULLETIN

The morning news flashed -

Breaking News: A flesh racket busted in Delhi Jail. Charge sheet filed against the Jail Superintendent and the Jailor.

The media had been broadcasting the news on a large scale, giving away whatever details they had. It had been an uncommon and rare scenario with respect to the watchdogs for society. A protector had become a devourer. There were talks, sessions, prime time debates and much more streaming on with respected lawyers and big shot politicians, as well as women's rights activists. Twitter had been fully utilized with tweets and re-tweets adding up to big data clouds. Amongst these, the names that were acclaimed included Commissioner of Police, Mr. Singhal and Crime Branch Inspector, Mr. Abhimanyu. Along with them, with triumphant exultation, the ovation recipients were Ishita, Lavanya and Gayatri and of course, the boys.

Lavanya, Gayatri, and Ishita were getting ready to catch their flights back to their dwelling. They were sending fond goodbyes, au revoir and adieu to each other. In the back of their minds, a sense of splendid feeling was running through, about where they were and how things got in place for them to perform such a stupendous task. There definitely had been some karmic cycle that brought them together. All the three women got so attached to each other, they promised to stay in touch forever.

The drowning sun was spreading pastel illumination across the sky. The birds were chirping and floating between the clouds in groups. The clouds showed a silver shine like a crown after a victory. The after feels were very positive and soothing.

Ishita had been soothing her eyes with such an aura of nature along with the cool evening breeze over her face while keeping her face out from the car window which Amit was driving.

Lavanya was standing at the airport lounge and viewing the beauty and strength of nature while witnessing the take offs of the flights to various destinations.

The manifestation of this nature's true image has also been evidenced by Gayatri in her scope of joyous victory. There has been definitely a fortunate stroke of serendipity, the destiny that had brought the three women together. By this time, they had developed a love and care for each other and an untold promise to support each other for times to come.

They were now a completely different person; and understood the purpose of their life. Being responsible, brave and aware gave them a sense of power the women thrived on.

Aristotle teaches that each man's life has a purpose and that the function of one's life is to attain that purpose. And when you understand that you really are above all pains and misfortune. The jewel that would cherish you is your smile.

3 months later...

Lavanya was in her office cabin. The Shubh-Labh Jewellery showroom has been adequately filled up with morning crowd. The glass cabin was situated at the far end of the ground floor. She was sitting with two of her designers and was engrossed in an intense discussion over jewellery designs for the next year release when her phone rang.

'Ma'am, your phone is ringing.' One of her colleagues

interrupted when she failed to observe it.

'Let it be...' Lavanya was so engrossed that she did not want to pick it up.

The phone again rang. She ignored. It rang a third time.

Furious Lavanya picked up the call and shouted, *'What?'* without looking at her phone screen.

At once, she calmed down, her face glowed up, her eyes twinkled and there was a smile on her face. She mouthed an excuse me to the team and walked out of the cabin and straight outside of the showroom.

'Hi Ishita, how are you?' Lavanya spoke up.

'She had a vision again, Gayatri called me. Are you free to discuss?'